AUTHOR'S NOTE

When I was a kid, one of my favorite TV shows was *Star Trek*—where Captain Kirk, Mr. Spock, and the rest of the *Enterprise* crew beamed down to different planets by stepping into the Transporter.

In *Following Baxter*, Professor Reese invents a teleporter after she discovers T-waves.

But can scientists teleport things in real life? It turns out they can—sort of.

Scientists can pair up two atoms (let's call them A and B), measure the properties of A (such as its energy and motion), and send that information to B, turning it into an exact copy of A.

During the process of measuring, the original A is destroyed, but a new A exists in a new location. In a sense, A has traveled from one location to another without physically moving through the space in between.

Does that mean that people will one day be able to teleport? Figuring out how to do it wouldn't be easy. After all, the human body is made up of trillions of atoms. Scientists would need to come up with a good way to measure and send all that information.

And that's not the only challenge. What about a person's memories, personality, likes and dislikes? Scientists would need to come up with a way to send that information, too.

There's another big question scientists wonder about: If during teleportation, original atoms are destroyed and an exact copy is created, does that mean if you teleported, you'd become a clone of yourself? Would you still be you?

There are a lot of questions still to be answered in the science of teleportation. But one thing is clear. There will be lots of opportunities in the years ahead for new scientists to join in.

FOLLOWING BAXTER

FOLLOWING BAXTER

Barbara Kerley

Illustrations by Gilbert Ford

HARPER
An Imprint of HarperCollinsPublishers

Following Baxter
Text copyright © 2018 by Barbara Kerley
Illustrations copyright © 2018 by Gilbert Ford
All rights reserved. Printed in the United States of America.

Library of Congress Control Number: 2017943440
ISBN 978-0-06-249978-3

Typography by Rick Farley
18 19 20 21 22   CG/LSCH   10 9 8 7 6 5 4 3 2 1

First Edition

For Scott—
and our magical dog, Seamus

CONTENTS

THE BIG WHITE MOVING VAN

When the big white moving van rumbled up to the house next door, I dumped my Crispy Rice down the kitchen sink and ran into my brother TJ's room.

"Wake up!" I pulled his pillow out from under his head and whapped his nose with it. "Someone's moving in next door!"

"Go away!"

I ran outside.

I'd been waiting forever for someone to move in, ever since the *For Sale* sign went up last summer. Then the sign changed to *Pending*, which Mom said meant "waiting," and I *had* been, for two months, even after it changed to *Sold*.

Considering how close together all the houses are in our

neighborhood, you'd think I might have noticed someone clomping up the old wooden porch steps next door and opening their front door. But Crispy Rice crackles a lot, so it's easy to miss something.

You couldn't miss the van, though. It was huge. A big guy with a bushy dark beard and ponytail got out and walked toward the house with a clipboard while another big guy with his head shaved smooth as an egg got out and stretched. They were sort of funny together because one was so hairy and one wasn't at all.

I leaned against the little fence between the two yards, waiting to see who was moving in. Maybe it was a family with a girl my age, so I wouldn't be stuck every afternoon with just TJ. Or a young couple with a baby they'd let me push in a stroller.

Instead, out walked an old lady wearing a Portland Trail Blazers T-shirt tucked into her elastic-waist jeans. Her short gray hair kind of stuck up on one side, like she'd forgotten to brush it. I reached up to check if I'd brushed mine.

The old lady talked to the clipboard guy while the egg-head guy pulled up the back hatch of the van. Then she noticed me and waved.

I waved back and thought, Oh well, no kids.

But at least I could see what kind of furniture the old lady had, because if she was rich, maybe she had her own pin-ball machine. I've seen that in movies. Or a grand piano, and then I could watch the two guys try to carry it up the porch steps and through the front door.

Suddenly, this big shaggy gray dog burst out of the house.

I thought, A dog! That's even better than a baby!

He bounded down the old lady's front walk, like he had springs on the bottoms of his feet. He bounced up the ramp into the moving van and back down the ramp and across the yard and over the fence, circling my legs before bounding back over the fence again. He tumbled to a stop right by the old lady, woofing the whole time. But he wasn't woofing in a scary way—he was woofing like he was saying how happy he was to be here and how happy he was that we were all here, too.

The old lady hurried into her house and came back out, holding a leash. The dog followed her over to the tree right across the fence from me. "He must have gotten out of the bathroom," she said, smiling at me. "I think I need to tie him up for a little while so he doesn't trip someone carry-ing furniture into the house."

"I can watch him!"

"Really? Thank you. That would be most helpful."

The dog stood beside her, quietly panting.

"What's his name?" I asked.

"Um, Buddy . . ." Then she shook her head. "No, wait—Charlie. Sammy? . . . Oh, this is terrible, but I can't remember." She rubbed her chin with her hand. "I think I wrote it down somewhere, but everything's in boxes right now."

"You don't know your own dog's name?"

"Well, he's not actually my dog. He belongs to a colleague at work. I'm only watching him for a few days."

The dog leaned his head against her hip and looked up at her, his long pink tongue flopped out and resting on his teeth.

"He sure *acts* like he's your dog," I said.

The lady laughed. "Yes, I suppose he does." She patted the dog's head. "You're sure you don't mind watching him?"

"No problem!" I clapped my hands on my thighs, and before I could say "Here, boy!" he jumped back over the fence and landed at my feet.

The lady laughed again. "What's your name, dear?"

"Jordie Marie Wallace." (I always put the middle name in, too, because it sounds so pretty all in a row like that.)

"Thank you, Jordie." She hurried toward her house.

I scritched under the dog's chin. "Hey, buddy!"

He reared up on his hind legs and planted his front paws on my shoulders, so fast and heavy it practically knocked me over. We stood eye to eye then, with his crazy silver eyebrows standing straight up and his black lips open, panting dog breath, and his shaggy gray beard, dripping water. Either he drooled a lot, or he'd already drunk from the old lady's toilet. "You're a good boy!" I nodded.

The dog nodded back.

Huh, I thought.

He dropped to the ground and leaned against me.

"Oh, by the way," the old lady called from across the yard, "I'm Professor Reese. Like the peanut butter cup."

And just as I started thinking how strange it was for someone to introduce herself like a candy bar and add a "Professor" in front of it, I also started noticing that the stuff coming out of the moving van was strange, too.

There was a huge wooden crate as big as a body with the word *Fragile* stamped on it a dozen times. There was a gray metal electronic "console"—that's what the egg-head guy called it—covered with lights and buttons. It was so heavy both guys grunted as they carried it up the porch steps. There were long skinny boxes, and tall skinnier boxes, and big coils of cable, and three computer monitors. The moving guys kept asking, "Where does this go?" and every time, Professor Reese's answer got more interesting.

Because every time they asked, Professor Reese answered, "The lab."

TJ VS. THE DOG

I sat down in the grass, and the dog settled next to me, giving a big sigh when I started to scratch his ribs.

Then TJ came outside eating a bagel with cream cheese. (He's a year younger but almost as tall as I am, which is really annoying.) "So, who's moving in—"

The dog jumped up and bounded toward him, woofing. TJ yelped, threw the bagel, and ran back inside, slamming our door behind him.

TJ's scared of big dogs, but I figured once he actually met this one, he'd like him. So I went over to the door, and the dog came with me. (After he ate the bagel.)

There was TJ, with his hands cupped around his eyes, peering through the window part in the door and making the glass fog up.

I heard the bolt slide closed. "Unlock the door, TJ!"

"No!"

I rang the doorbell three times, until Mom answered in her pajamas. "What's going on?" she asked as TJ ran back toward the kitchen.

We're not allowed to have a dog. Mom's asked the landlord—twice. But he's what Mom calls a "sour old crank" and said no the second time, too. He said he wouldn't even let us have a dog if it slept in a doghouse in the yard. He had a NO DOG POLICY.

So Mom couldn't let the dog in the house, which was just as well seeing as how we probably would have had to peel TJ off the kitchen ceiling.

She scooted out to sit on our porch steps. The dog stood with his front paws on the bottom step, looking up at us.

I told Mom about Professor Reese watching the dog for a few days, and all the strange things going into her lab (which we agreed was weird because who has a lab in their *house*, and what did it used to be, the dining room?). "But she's really nice."

Mom kissed the top of my head and patted the top of the dog's. "I have some blueberries in the freezer. How about I make some muffins for us to take over?"

"OK!"

When Mom opened the front door, TJ slid out about halfway, which made me think he must have been watching us the whole time.

The dog looked at TJ and swished his tail back and forth.

"He's really sweet," I said.

"Humph," TJ replied.

I patted the spot next to me. The dog scrambled up the steps and plopped down, his bony elbows clunking on the porch. I scritched the coarse gray hair on the back of his neck and the softer hair between his crazy eyebrows, and he rolled over into me.

TJ kept the door open, so he could dive back into the house, I guess. But by then I was stroking the tiny hairs on the bridge of the dog's nose and his long ears, soft as velvet, and he had closed his eyes.

"So the lady moving in is a professor," I said. "She has a lab in her house."

TJ scrunched up his eyebrows. "Weird."

"I know."

We sat watching the moving van guys. After a while, the dog started to snore. The smell of warm blueberry muffins floated out our doorway, and everything was perfect.

Then no more boxes came out of the van. The egg-head guy pulled down the rattly back hatch, which woke the dog. When the two guys got in the van and slammed their doors, he jumped to his feet. Mom came out in her jeans and T-shirt, holding a big plate.

She handed it to me. The plate was warmed by the stack of muffins, and she'd added a packet of peppermint tea. I decided that when I was a mom, I'd make welcome muffins for new neighbors, too.

"Ready?" Mom asked.

The dog followed me down the stairs, sniffing like crazy. But TJ hung behind. "Come on, TJ!" I said. "He's not even looking at you!"

"Yeah, right," he grumbled, but then he came, too. Even though he's scared of big dogs, TJ hates to miss anything. Also, Mom's muffins are really good.

We climbed the stairs to Professor Reese's front porch. "Hello!" Mom called into the open doorway.

Professor Reese hurried out from the back. "Hi, Jordie. I was just coming to get our mutual friend. Thank you again."

"These are for you." I held out the plate. "Welcome to the neighborhood."

"Oh my! They look delicious!" Professor Reese said. "My table and chairs are all set up. Please come in."

"I'm sure you're busy," Mom said. "We just—"

"OK!" I said before she could mess it up. Even if you are busy, you should never be too busy for blueberry muffins.

Besides, I wanted to see the lab.

I stepped into the living room past boxes stacked every-where. Professor Reese had a purple couch and an orange armchair. "You have an orange chair!" I said because all our furniture is brown.

She winked. "I like bright colors." She led us into the dining room, which meant the lab must be somewhere else. "I'll put on the kettle. I know just what box it's in."

TJ stopped in front of a stack of pictures leaning against the dining table. The first one was a gigantic blue wave, towering up to curl over a little fishing boat. He shook his head. "The guys in that boat are toast."

Professor Reese laughed. "I got that one in Tokyo. I have prints from all over the world. Take a look while I make the tea." She headed into the kitchen.

We looked at the prints of markets and rivers and people and tried to guess where they were from. Mom thought maybe France and Russia and somewhere in South America. I wondered what it would be like to go to all those places. Then the kettle whistled, and Professor Reese brought in a yellow teapot and four yellow cups.

We all sat down at the dining table. The dog flopped in the corner like he'd been living in the house his whole life. And TJ just scowled down at his muffin because every time he looked up, the dog was panting, watching him eat.

Mom and Professor Reese did that thing grown-ups do, asking about each other's jobs—like how Mom worked in a doctor's office billing insurance, and Professor Reese taught physics at the university and served as an adviser to the science museum.

"So you have a lab in your house?" I asked.

"I will." Professor Reese nodded. "I'm setting it up in the basement."

"Can we see it?"

She shrugged. "There's nothing to see. It's just a room full of boxes right now."

"Speaking of boxes, we should let you unpack." Mom pushed back her chair.

I broke off a piece of my muffin and held it out to the dog. He gobbled it up. "Did you remember the dog's name yet?" I asked Professor Reese.

She laughed. "No. I can email his former owner, but he's flying to Dubai today."

"I can't believe you're watching a friend's dog on your moving day!" Mom said.

"Well, it was an emergency." Professor Reese explained that her friend got a new job at a university in Dubai. He decided it was too hot there to take the dog, so he found a great family in Portland to adopt him. "Then, at the last minute, they changed their minds." Professor Reese shook

her head. "He was in a panic when he came into work yesterday. So I said I would take care of the dog until I could find a good home for him."

I looked around the room. "*This* looks like a good home."

"Oh, I'm much too busy for a dog, Jordie."

Darn, I thought.

"But that reminds me," Professor Reese said. "Is there a veterinarian in walking distance? I don't own a car."

"I can show you!" I said. "Me and TJ can go."

He looked at me like, *Wait, what?*

Mom frowned, the tiniest bit. "Well, uh—"

"Sure! It's on the way to the music store where Dad works, and me and TJ walk there all the time," I said mostly to remind Mom. "And Mom always says it's nice to help your neighbors," I added, so she'd say yes.

So Professor Reese put the rest of the muffins on the kitchen counter. Then me, TJ, and Professor Reese headed out, with me holding the dog leash and TJ staying as far away from the dog as he could.

Everyone noticed us—Mr. Hutchins, out pruning his hedges, and Mrs. Wesley, walking her poodle, Moxie, and even Tyler from my class, who was shooting hoops at the park. The whole street noticed because you couldn't help but pay attention to a dog like that:

"Oh my gosh, your dog is cute!"

"He's so big!"

"He's so sweet-tempered!" ("Yeah, right," said TJ.)

When we got to the vet's, Professor Reese went over to look at all the flyers stuck on the bulletin board. "I need to find a dog walker to start on Monday until I can find a home for him."

"I can walk him!" I said.

"I need a professional—someone I can count on, every afternoon."

"You can count on me! All I do after school is get stuck with TJ!"

"Hey!" he cried.

"Please?" I added. "I really love dogs, and we're not allowed to have one."

"Well, you can ask your mom." She tore off a strip of paper with a phone number from a dog-walker flyer. "I'll bring this home, in case she says no."

"She won't say no," I said. I swallowed, hard. I didn't actually know that for sure. Me and TJ got out of school at two thirty. We had to walk straight home—and stay there—until Mom got home from work about four.

I *might* be able to convince her, but only if I could convince TJ to go with me.

When we got back to Professor Reese's kitchen, she found the box with glasses and bowls. She got us some water and the dog some water. Then he plopped down, his beard puddling water where he rested his chin.

"I wonder what his name is," I said.

"I don't know if it really matters," Professor Reese said. "Whoever adopts him will probably want to give him a new name."

"Killer," TJ suggested. "Or Wolf."

"You know," Professor Reese said, "he reminds me a bit of my great-uncle Baxter. He had a beard like that. And those muttonchop sideburns. And, come to think of it, the same bushy eyebrows." The dog's eyebrows went up and down, first the left, then the right, as he looked at each of us in turn.

I petted the dog's head, and he turned his face up toward me.

"You're a good boy!" I smiled.

He pulled the corners of his cheeks up, like he was grinning back at me.

"Hey!" I looked up to see if they had seen it, but Professor Reese was putting the rest of the glasses in a cupboard while TJ grabbed another muffin from the plate.

I turned back to the dog, but he just flopped down and rolled onto his side.

"Run upstairs, Jordie, and see if you can find a box marked *Dog Bed* in the master bedroom," Professor Reese said. "We can't have Baxter sleeping on the floor."

3

AN AWFUL LOT
OF WAFFLES

The next morning, I woke up before everyone, and it was really boring with just me awake. It was so boring that I couldn't imagine how much more boring it must be when I was asleep, so I was glad I slept through that part.

It was good I woke up early. I had a lot to figure out. I had to convince TJ to walk Baxter with me on Monday and convince Mom to say yes.

I walked into the kitchen for some orange juice, but when I poured it, a little splashed out. I leaned down and slurped it off the countertop.

That was a trick I'd figured out after last year's parent-teacher conference, when Mom came home saying the teacher wanted me to look for "opportunities to be more

15

dependable." Mom thought cleaning up when I spilled was a *great* opportunity.

In fact, Mom didn't nag me about anything anymore. She just said, "What a great opportunity . . ." and I knew I had to do whatever the naggy thing was.

Suddenly, I thought, That's it!

Walking Baxter would be the perfect opportunity because Professor Reese was depending on me. Mom would love it!

As for TJ, I'd try to convince him how fun dog walking would be. And I'd say it like *Fun!*—with a capital *F* and an exclamation point.

But if that didn't work, there was always a bribe.

I finished my juice and hurried back to my room, which was a big fat opportunity, too. There were books and papers and clothes all over the floor, and that was a problem.

Every Sunday, me and TJ had to clean our rooms so Mom could vacuum after she read the paper. If our rooms were too messy, then *we* had to vacuum, which was worse.

I scooped up the papers and stuffed them into the recycling bin in the kitchen because I was pretty sure they weren't homework. I figured some clothes were clean and some were dirty, so I split it half in the drawers and half in the laundry hamper.

But I was always careful when I lined up my books-for-being-a-vet-one-day. I had books on cats, birds, hamsters, gerbils, rabbits, horses, and even one on elephants (because you never know). But my favorites were my four dog books. Now that Baxter was staying next door, I'd need to read them even more.

I grabbed the biggest one, ran into TJ's room, and plopped down on the end of his bed. If I read loud enough, maybe he'd get up and the *Fun!* could begin.

TJ liked gross, goopy stuff, so I started there. "'Common Dog Ailments—'"

"Go away!" He rolled over and buried his face under his armpit.

I read out loud about bloat and then mange. By the time I got to heartworm (which is seriously gross and probably a little goopy, too, because *worms* crawl around inside your *heart*), TJ was saying, "Eww!"

I slammed the book shut. "Let's go see Baxter this morning! It'll be *Fun!*"

"I need to work on my short."

TJ was using LEGOs to make a stop-motion short. (The *short* was short for "short movie." But since it took eight pictures to make *one second* of film, for a thirty-second film he needed 240 pictures, which didn't sound short to me at all.) He was learning how to make it in the Video Club at school, which met once a week during lunch. The club was planning a schoolwide Movie Night where families could

come, and there would be popcorn, even. But that wasn't for a while yet. "You still have three weeks," I said.

"I only have fifty-one pictures so far. That's only six point four seconds."

"If we hang out with Baxter this morning, you can work on it all afternoon."

"No."

"TJ, please? It'll be *Fun!*"

"No." He headed for the bathroom.

My shoulders slumped. I slid like a wet noodle down off the bed and landed on his sweatshirt, which was lying on the floor.

Darn, I thought. There was only one bribe I could think of that didn't cost money.

When he came back into his room to get dressed, I said, "How about I clean your room, and after breakfast, we go see Baxter."

"You'll clean my room good enough for Mom to vacuum?"

"But we have to stay for a while and take him for a walk."

He shrugged. "OK." He grabbed his clothes and went back into the bathroom to change.

I looked around and groaned. There were papers and clothes and books all over the place, plus a million blue and yellow and red and green LEGO pieces sprinkled everywhere, like his room was a big sloppy cupcake. Mom was always vacuuming up the littlest ones when she pushed the sucking part under his bed. As soon as he heard them clattering up the hose, he'd get mad. She'd get mad that he was mad and say that he should have cleaned better. By then, I usually went out to the front porch with a book because, *seriously*.

I put TJ's papers on his desk. I piled up his clothes to put in the hamper because I figured they were probably all dirty. I stuffed his books and comic books in his bookcase. Then I crawled around, reaching under furniture to pick up every single stupid LEGO piece.

When TJ came out of the bathroom, I dumped his clothes in the hamper, and we ran over to Dad's for breakfast.

Mom and Dad are separated, but we all still live together. Sort of. Dad's part of the house is a studio apartment built right on top of the garage. Four years ago, when he and Mom were fighting a lot, he moved out there one weekend to "cool off" and then just ended up staying there.

My best friend Megan thinks it's weird, but it happened so long ago that it just seems normal to me. Besides, as Dad always says, "It could be worse." And he's right—because even though they're separated, I get to see him all the time. (Which is actually more than Megan sees her dad, who lives an hour away and she only sees every other weekend.)

Plus, Mom and Dad hardly ever fight anymore.

We ran up the steps on the side of the garage and into his studio. Dad was at his little kitchen counter, which had a sink, a microwave, and a minirefrigerator. He didn't cook much, but waffles were his specialty, and he made them for us every Sunday—not the toaster kind, the *real* kind made in a real waffle iron he kept in the cupboard especially for us.

He was mixing the batter when we came in. "Just in time," he said as he poured batter onto the waffle iron and brought the lid down.

I told Dad all about Baxter as the batter puffed up under the lid, baking toasty brown. Dad forked the waffle onto a plate and handed it to TJ, who slathered on peanut butter, squeezed syrup on top, and dug in.

"It was so *Fun!* taking Baxter on a walk yesterday," I said. "Wasn't it, TJ?"

"Mmpfh." His cheeks were too full to answer. He wandered over to turn on the TV. He and Dad were always watching crazy movies about spaceships fighting each other with all sorts of crazy equipment, like lasers and weird flashing torpedoes. TJ made the sound effects right along with the movie. It was even worse when he was eating waffles because his sound effects got sticky with syrup and splattered everywhere, so I sat as far away as possible.

Dad put a fresh waffle onto another plate and handed it to me. "Baxter sounds like quite a dog."

"He is," I agreed. "I can't wait for you to meet him!"

I was full after a waffle and a half. But it took TJ forever to stop eating, and by then, I could hardly wait to see Baxter.

I clicked off the TV and dragged TJ home. "Can we go over and see if Professor Reese needs help with Baxter while she unpacks?" I asked Mom. "Our rooms are already clean."

She looked up from her newspaper. "That's a nice change. Sure."

So I ran over to Professor Reese's house with TJ shuffling after me.

When I rang the doorbell, Baxter started woofing. TJ must have thought it was the kind of woofing like, *Go away, there's an attack dog behind this door*. He wouldn't even come up the steps. But I knew it was the kind of woofing like, *Yay, someone's here, let's see who it is*.

Professor Reese opened the door. "I'm glad you're here. I need your help. Come on in for a minute." She walked back into the living room.

"OK!" I petted Baxter's head as he looked up at me. "You're a good boy!"

I nodded, and he nodded back.

I turned to TJ. "Did you see that? Come closer and let him put his paws on your shoulders."

"What are you, crazy?"

"After you see eye to eye, he'll nod to you, too." I turned to Baxter. "Right?"

I nodded, and he nodded back.

"He's just doing what you do," TJ said.

"No, he's not! He understands me! Right, Baxter?"

We both nodded again.

TJ shrugged. "Whatever, Jordie." Then he scooted behind me and into the house.

Professor Reese showed us the flyers she'd made with Baxter's picture. They said, *Free to a Good Home*, only I realized they should say, *Free to a REALLY Good Home*. So we fixed them and then walked around the park, putting them up. We even put one up next to the basketball courts at the park, where Tyler from my class was shooting hoops (which is what he seemed to do in his spare time when he wasn't getting in trouble with the teacher, which is what I mainly saw him do).

We put flyers up all over the neighborhood, and the whole time, I was not-so-secretly hoping that it wouldn't work.

Because Baxter was perfect, and he was right next door. He was the closest thing to having my own dog I could have without having one, which I couldn't.

When we got back, I said, "Would you like us to take care of Baxter while you set up your lab?"

"Why, yes," Professor Reese said. "That would be very helpful."

So we all trooped down to the basement.

There were desks and tables and shelves, all made out of gray metal. The file cabinets had drawers that screeched when you opened them.

I wasn't sure how long TJ would stay, since technically we'd finished the walk and helping her in the lab was extra. But he discovered that in addition to two normal chairs, Professor Reese had a black rolling desk chair. He sat down and spun around. Fast.

"You're going to barf up your peanut butter waffles," I said.

"No, I'm not." He kicked off with his feet to spin faster.

Professor Reese crawled around on the floor, running cables everywhere, hooking up all three computers to the big electronic console (with lights and buttons).

I started putting physics and math books on the shelves, keeping Baxter at my side. Whenever he walked toward TJ, I'd call him back, because TJ was finally forgetting he was scared of big dogs. I didn't want Baxter's "exuberance," as Professor Reese put it, to remind TJ up the stairs and out the front door.

But as long as Baxter stayed with me, TJ was fine. Besides, he'd discovered the little lever under the seat that made it go up and down. "Dude, watch this!" He spun around and made the seat go down. Then he tried to spin around and make it go up, which was hard because you had to sort of stand up and get your weight off the seat. TJ couldn't figure out a way to simultaneously spin around in the chair and stand up out of it. Though he tried for a while.

So everything was OK.

Me and Professor Reese worked our way through the stacks of cardboard boxes filling the corner. She opened one box and pulled out a bright red hat, which she put on top of the bookcase. We pulled manila folders out of the other boxes to put in her filing cabinets. But when the stacks of boxes got low enough, I saw a strange piece of equipment pushed up against the wall. From the size of it, I guessed it must have been what was in the body-sized crate that the moving guys carried in.

I thought, What *is* that?

Then I stepped closer to get a better look.

4

THE BODY-SIZED CRATE

The strange piece of equipment was long, red, and plastic, with a lid that could curve down over the top like a coffin. It reminded me of a weird bench, or maybe a skinny bed, only it couldn't be a bed because it didn't have a mattress. It had thin metal rods lined up side by side (where the mattress wasn't) and more rods inside the top (where there wouldn't be a mattress anyway). The whole thing looked very uncomfortable, like if you tried to sleep in Dad's waffle iron with the lid down, and why would you do that?

"What's this big red thing?" I asked.

"It used to be a sixteen-lamp home tanning bed," Professor Reese said.

"What does it do now?"

"I'm still figuring that out." She walked to a shelf and picked up a long cardboard tube labeled *Do Not Bend*. She slid out a roll of posters. "Could you help me hang these, dear? The lab won't feel like home without them."

All three posters were the same drawing of the Electromagnetic Spectrum: a long thin band of different colors, like a rainbow, going red-orange-yellow-green-blue-indigo-violet, one color fading into the next.

"Oh, that's pretty," I said.

"It is pretty." Professor Reese nodded. "And it's pretty darn important. This is the range of electromagnetic radiation— from radio waves all the way down to gamma rays."

There were a bunch of other waves, too, like X-rays (for seeing skeletons) and microwaves (for making popcorn).

TJ stopped spinning in the chair. "What are all the numbers for?" He liked numbers, and the spectrum was covered with them, like ten with a little three next to it, or ten with a little negative twelve.

"They show the length of the various waves. Ten to the third meters is ten times ten times ten—that's longer than ten football fields, end to end. But ten to the negative twelfth is smaller than an atom."

"Oh." He kicked off to spin the chair again.

At first I thought if I were decorating a room, I would choose rainbow posters without all the numbers. But then

I thought, maybe if you're a physicist then a rainbow is pretty, but ten to the negative twelfth is pretty, too.

"So why do you have three copies of the same poster?" I asked.

"You'll see."

She had me hold the first poster against the wall while she taped it up.

"It looks crooked," TJ chimed in, but me and Professor Reese ignored him because by then his eyeballs were spinning around more than the chair.

The second poster Professor Reese wanted to hang sideways, with the radio waves on the bottom and the gamma rays at the top. And even though the numbers were sideways, she didn't care. The third poster she wanted to hang completely upside down, and then of course the numbers were upside down, too.

"I've found as a scientist that I learn a lot by looking at things from a different angle." She smiled. "Try turning a world map upside down sometime and make South America on top and North America on the bottom—"

"Can you *do* that?" I asked.

"You can, and you should. After all, there is no right side up in space."

I stared at the posters, thinking about how we could be upside down at that *very moment* without even realizing

it, only at the same time there being no such thing as upside down. I was thinking so hard that it took a second to notice the strange gurgling sound coming from behind me. When I turned around, this is what I saw:

TJ, with his eyeballs still spinning around in his head, leaning as far back in the seat as he could. And Baxter with his front paws up on the armrests (one paw on each side of TJ). Because the chair was still slowly spinning, Baxter was sort of walking around with it, sidestepping on his hind feet.

It certainly gave me an opportunity to look at something from a lot of different angles.

Baxter started panting. He leaned in so close his face was almost touching TJ's, which looked a little green.

"Baxter's just saying hi," I told TJ.

"Gaaahhh . . ." TJ gurgled. He didn't seem to realize that you could tell, if you would just calm down for a minute, that even though all of Baxter's teeth were showing, his black lips were *smiling*, and you could tell that because the long shaggy tail at the other end was wagging. But I guess TJ couldn't see that, as there was a lot of Baxter in between.

"He's *smiling*," I said.

"Nuhhhh!" TJ moaned back, which made Baxter start making his own little moaning noises in a nice friendly way, as the chair spun slowly around.

"Oh my!" Professor Reese exclaimed.

You could tell the moaning (Baxter's, not TJ's) wasn't growling if you just stopped to listen to it. But TJ was too busy making his own noises to be listening to anyone else's, including mine.

Baxter slowly raised a paw to put on TJ's shoulder—

"He just wants to see eye to eye," I tried to explain.

But TJ lurched the chair back, Baxter fell in his lap, the chair tipped over (with TJ still in it), and Baxter landed completely on top.

"Ahhh!" TJ scrambled free. He ran up the stairs and out the front door. Just like I thought he would.

I groaned. How was I going to convince TJ to go dog walking *now*? "I think I need to go home."

"Come by in the morning before school, and I'll show you where I hid the key," Professor Reese said. "You checked with your mom about walking Baxter?"

"I can do it," I said (which was technically true—I would do a great job as a dog walker). I hugged Baxter around the tummy and noodled his ears and went home, thinking it was impossible that anyone else could love Baxter as much as I did.

When I got home, I found TJ at his desk, the hood of his hoodie pulled up over his head. He was working on his

LEGO short. "Don't. Say. Anything."

I plopped down on his bed. I knew there was no way I could convince him by tomorrow that dog walking would be *Fun!* And his room was still clean. I needed a bigger bribe—because Professor Reese needed a dog walker for *days*.

I sat thinking, watching TJ work.

The actors for the short were two LEGO figures I'd just given him for his ninth birthday. They were the kind of figures that came sealed in a bag, so I couldn't tell which ones I was buying. TJ had been excited when he opened the first bag and it was a caveman with a big club, but the second bag was a cheerleader—and he wasn't excited about *her* at all.

But later he figured out if he took red and green Magic Markers and added gore and goop to her face, he could make her a zombie cheerleader. And then it was OK.

So his short was going to be an epic battle between Caveman and Zombie Cheerleader.

Right now, Caveman was running step by step (which meant picture by picture) across the desktop, past little LEGO buildings. Caveman didn't know yet that Zombie Cheerleader was hiding behind one of them, waiting to jump out and clobber him over the head with her pompom and then eat his LEGO brains.

"Your short is going to be so good," I said.

"Um-hm," he grunted. He moved Caveman's foot forward and snapped a picture.

"It's going to be really funny when they start fighting."

"Why are you in here?" He moved the other foot. "You always say how boring it is to watch me do this."

I've noticed with TJ that sometimes it works best when I just tell him the truth. "I'm trying to figure out what to bribe you with so you'll go dog walking with me after school tomorrow. I don't think Mom will let me go by myself."

He thought for a minute. "All my chores after dinner tonight."

I sighed because that was a lot. Mom always said that since she cooked, we had to clean up. After dinner, she went into the living room to relax with a book, while me and TJ split the work: wiping the counters, loading the dishwasher, and sweeping the kitchen floor.

Doing the whole thing would be a lot. But Baxter was worth it.

"OK. Deal."

So after dinner, Mom went into the living room, and TJ leaned back in his chair and put his feet up on the kitchen table. "This is the life." He grinned.

As I was doing all the stupid chores, I decided to convince

Mom about the dog walking after she'd had her long hot bath. She was always relaxed after that.

While Mom took her bath, I sat on my bed with all my dog books. I wanted to figure out what kind of dog Baxter was.

I opened up all four books to the section on dog breeds and studied the pictures.

Baxter was the size and color of a Scottish deerhound, and he had their crazy silver eyebrows and scruffy beard, too. But he had a strong, shaggy tail more like a flat-coated retriever. His ears were long and floppy like a wirehaired vizsla. And his bushy mustache and "muttonchop side-burns," as Professor Reese had called them, looked more like a Glen of Imaal terrier.

Deerhounds were smart, the books said. Retrievers were cheerful. Vizslas were energetic. And Glen of Imaal terriers were good with kids.

All of which sounded just like Baxter.

Mom came in to kiss me good night.

"You know how I'm supposed to look for opportunities to be dependable?" I said. I told her why walking Baxter would do that plus how *Fun!* TJ thought it would be and how we'd stay together the whole time and stay in the neighborhood, too.

"I can see you've given this a lot of thought." She nodded.

"There's one thing I'm worried about, though."

"We'll be really careful! We'll look both ways before crossing the street!"

"What I'm worried about is you getting too attached to Baxter." She patted my arm. "You know Professor Reese isn't going to keep him, honey."

"I know. It's just for a few days. But please, Mom? I really want to!"

"OK. We can give it a try."

Yes!

Mom kissed me good night and went back to her room.

I looked out my window toward Professor Reese's house. There was a light on in the living room, but I figured Baxter was down in the lab with her because it looked like Professor Reese was working late: the basement window was glowing.

But the weird thing was, the light coming from the window was *red*.

The red light grew brighter and brighter, like maybe she was turning on the equipment, piece by piece—even the tanning bed that used to be a tanning bed—growing redder and redder until suddenly . . .

The house went dark.

7:15 ON THE NOSE

In the morning, I walked into TJ's room to wake him up. He was lying on his stomach with the blanket all wadded up beneath him and his arms thrown over his head—sort of like if Superman was flying and crash-landed in a basket of laundry. His pillow had slid to the floor from the force of the impact.

I tapped my finger on the back of his head. "Anybody home?"

He swatted at me. "Go away!"

TJ's blanket wadded up made me think he'd had a nightmare, where he was fighting snarling wolf dogs with black lips. So I left the rest of the Crispy Rice for him and ate Wheat Flakes instead, which taste OK, only they don't talk to you while you eat them.

Mom was in her room, getting dressed for work. As soon as I finished eating, I yelled, "Can I go see Baxter now?"

"It's too early. You can stop by on your way to school."

I slumped against the counter. Then I remembered that I hadn't told Dad all about everything yet. "OK, I'm going to Dad's."

"Seven fifteen on the nose, Jordie. Watch Dad's clock," Mom yelled back. "And can you make sure TJ's awake?"

I went back into TJ's room, grabbed his hoodie from the floor, and threw it at him, because an atomic bomb could go off underneath the nightstand before he'd wake up, never mind an alarm clock. "Mom says get up!" Then I ran over to Dad's.

Dad works at the music store, selling guitars and ukuleles and banjos, but they don't open until ten, so he's always relaxed in the mornings.

He was sitting on the couch in a black T-shirt and blue jeans with his guitar on his lap and a cup of coffee on the floor by his bare feet. He nodded at me and kept playing.

I filled a mug with water and stuck it in the microwave to make hot chocolate.

Suddenly, I thought, *Microwaves* are heating up the water. I'd seen them on the posters in Professor Reese's lab, and now I knew they were part of the electromagnetic

spectrum and made the water hot enough to melt the floaty little marshmallows.

I'd never really thought about how the water got hot before—I'd always just pushed the start button.

I added the cocoa mix and then settled on the couch. I told Dad all about Professor Reese's lab and the lights going out.

"Hmm. A lot of older homes in our neighborhood have old wiring. She probably had a tripped circuit breaker," Dad said.

"What's that?" I asked.

"If you have too many things plugged in, it can overload the circuit. The circuit breaker trips to avoid overheating."

"But we have an old house, too," I said. "Our circuits never trip."

Dad shrugged. "She must have been trying to draw a whole lot of power."

"Huh," I said.

Then Dad's phone rang.

He winced. "It's Mom." He pushed the button and said, "A bright and shiny good morning!"

I thought, Uh-oh.

I looked over at Dad's clock. 7:21. I'd just blabbed my way through another great opportunity to be dependable.

"Uh-huh . . ." Dad said into the phone. "Seven fifteen on

the nose . . ." He cupped his palm over the mouthpiece and whispered to me, "Mom's mad at us."

I dumped my cup into his sink and ran back home because I've noticed if I get there before she hangs up, then she's annoyed at me but also annoyed at Dad who's still on the other end of the line. It's not as bad split up like that.

I shut the front door as quietly as possible and hurried to TJ's room because I've also noticed it looks like I'm not as late if I'm waiting for *him*.

He was in his room, setting up for the next picture of his short.

"Hurry up!" I said. "I want to say good morning to Baxter!"

"We still have three minutes."

"But I need to see where she hides the key. C'mon, TJ! We have a deal!"

"OK, OK!"

Mom was still talking to Dad. It was a good time to leave.

"TJ's finally ready," I yelled to Mom. "Bye!" I hustled him out the door and over to Professor Reese's.

TJ hung back on the sidewalk, but I went up and rang the doorbell. Baxter woofed *Hello hello hello hello* until Professor Reese opened the door in a yellow leotard and black footless tights. She kind of looked like a bumblebee except

she was holding a newspaper. "What's a six-letter 'tropical fruit,' Jordie?" she said, as Baxter pushed past her.

"What?" Then I saw that the newspaper was unfolded to the crossword puzzle. "Um, *banana*?" Baxter stuck his cold, wet nose in my hands. "Hi, Baxter!"

"Of course!" Professor Reese scribbled it in. "With all those *a*'s I kept thinking *papaya*, but the *y* didn't fit." She waved to TJ. He waved back.

Meanwhile, I was petting Baxter all over. He wagged not just his tail but his whole back half. He wagged so hard, he practically fell off his own back feet. Then he bounded down the walk toward TJ.

TJ swung his backpack off his back and held it in front of him like a shield or maybe a battering ram. "Sit! Stay! Heel!"

But Professor Reese gave a whistle before Baxter's exuberance had a chance to knock TJ over. Baxter came right back to her. "He is so smart," she told me (Baxter, not TJ). "While I do my morning crossword, I like to do yoga—the blood flow is good for the brain. And Baxter's been helping me. Every time I do a downward dog pose to help me figure out a word, he does upward dog, and our noses meet."

"I wish I could hang out all morning with Baxter." I fluffed up his crazy silver eyebrows to make them even crazier.

"Well, you have the next best thing: your mom called this morning to say it was OK for you and TJ to walk him after school."

"I can't wait!" I said, because even if Baxter slept at Professor Reese's house at night, if I took him for a walk during the day, he'd be half my dog.

"Let me show you where I hid the key," she said. "It's by the back door . . ." She led me around the side of the house, with Baxter coming, too, and TJ, not at all.

As we walked, I said, "I saw your lights go out last night."

She smiled. "I had too many things plugged into the same outlet in the lab."

"For your project that you're still figuring out?"

"Yep."

"Huh," I said.

"Ah, here we are," she said as we reached the back door. "The key's under the pink begonia," which, it turned out, was a flowerpot full of pink flowers.

I lifted the clay pot and there was the key. "OK."

I turned to Baxter and patted my shoulders. He reared up on his hind legs and planted his paws. "Ever since me and Baxter saw eye to eye on Saturday, he's understood me. Watch this!"

I smiled at Baxter. "I get to walk you after school!"

He grinned back.

"See, he's smiling!" I said.

"Interesting," Professor Reese said. "He appears to have highly developed mirror neurons."

"What's that?"

"They're special cells in the brain. Some scientists believe mirror neurons help infant animals learn from their parents," Professor Reese said. "They may help an animal understand the actions of another animal."

"TJ didn't believe me," I said to Baxter. "But I *knew* you understood me. Right?"

I nodded, and he nodded back.

Professor Reese laughed.

I eased Baxter's big paws off my shoulders. He dropped back to the ground. All three of us smiled the whole way back around to the front of the house, and then the only person not smiling was TJ.

He scowled the whole way to school, but I didn't care—we had a deal, so he had to go on the dog walk later.

When I got to the school playground, I ran to find Megan. I knew she'd be excited to hear about Baxter because when we grow up, we're going to open a vet/beauty parlor. I'll take care of the dogs and give them a bath, while she does the dog owners' hair at the same time. As Dad said when I told him our plan, it really will be a full-service salon.

I told her all about how cute Baxter was. "And I get to

take him on a walk this afternoon!"

"Aww! I wish my house was closer to your house—you could walk him over so I could meet him," she said.

I could tell Megan was jealous that there wasn't a Baxter living next door to her, which was nice for a change as usually I am the one being jealous. Megan gets to do a million lessons like piano and ballet and horseback riding. All I get to do in the afternoons is hang out with TJ (and you certainly don't need lessons for that).

"Ask your mom when you can come over!" I said. Then we ran over to the playground bars, where Aisha and Jasmine were waiting.

"Baxter is soooo cute!" I told them as we swung around backward on the bars.

Aisha hopped down from the bar and grabbed her notebook and pencil out of her backpack. "What does he look like?"

I described his silvery-gray fur and his long, long nose and crazy eyebrows, and she started trying to sketch Baxter. "Like this?" she asked.

"Oh! I forgot!" Jasmine hopped down, too. She unzipped her backpack and pulled out a plastic bag. "I tried a new recipe with my mom yesterday—cranberry-orange scones."

So we all munched on scones and watched Aisha try to match her dog sketch with my description, with me saying,

"I think his ears are a *little* longer," and, "His eyebrows are definitely *way* crazier!" and her erasing and redrawing the sketch until it almost looked just like him. "He *is* cute!" she said.

"Totally," I agreed.

Then Aisha closed the cover of her notebook, and Jasmine crumpled up the empty scone bag, and they both picked up their backpacks and started running toward the classroom.

"Where are you going?" I yelled.

"The bell rang. You didn't notice?" Megan swung her backpack up onto her shoulder and hurried after them.

Sure enough, the playground monitor was walking our way. I grabbed my backpack and caught up to Megan.

"Do you think your mom will let you come over tomorrow to meet him?" I asked.

"Maybe. I have a piano lesson. We're practicing for our recital."

But for once, I wasn't jealous, because now I had Baxter.

By the time we reached the classroom, our teacher, Mrs. Abernathy-Clarke (who the class calls Mrs. A.), was looking at the clock. But technically, we were sitting down as the tardy bell rang, so it was OK. All I needed to do was quickly finish telling Jasmine (to my left) and Aisha (to my right) about how swishy Baxter's tail was—

"Jordie."

—but Mrs. A. was already talking so much I wasn't even sure they could *hear* me. I whispered louder while Mrs. A. was writing on the overhead—

"*Jordie . . .*"

—because I just needed to add *one more thing* about how Baxter's ears felt as soft as velvet—

"JORDIE!"

—before I wrote down the big, long answer to question number three.

Mrs. A. seemed extra impatient all day, and I barely had time to tell Megan and Aisha and Jasmine everything else about Baxter during lunch and afternoon recess.

But then, at the end of recess, I suddenly had a terrible thought: What if some new family with a really good home had seen the flyers we put up? What if they'd called Professor Reese after I left for school and then rushed over to her house?

What if when Baxter saw them his whole back half wagged so hard he practically fell over? And then he ran to their car woofing *Hooray hooray hooray hooray* and never looked back?

What if when I got home from school, he was gone?

6

THE BUZZ, THE *POP!*, AND A LITTLE BIT OF SCREAMING

As soon as the bell rang, I didn't even wait for TJ, even though we're supposed to walk home together. I ran straight to Professor Reese's house.

I grabbed the key from under the potted pink begonia and unlocked the back door. I hurried through the kitchen and the dining room, but at the living room, I stopped short.

It looked like it could have been in a magazine. All the packing boxes were gone. Neat rows of books filled the bookcase. The black coffee table was completely empty except for a glass vase with a single white rose. The room smelled lemony clean, like nobody lived there (or at least, like TJ didn't live there). It was like a museum, only without the red velvet ropes to keep you out of the displays.

I thought, What if I knock something over? Or break something?

It looked like all the petals of the rose would come fluttering down if I even sneezed. I wasn't sure I belonged there—like I had to be quiet and careful.

"Baxter?" I said as carefully as I could.

A second later, I heard his toenails scrambling up the basement stairs.

He bounded out of the basement stairwell, his tail spinning a million times a minute. I dropped to my knees, held my arms wide open, and let him crash into me. "You're still here," I said into the fur on his neck as I petted and petted and petted him.

I sat back onto the floor, and Baxter climbed all over me, panting in my face.

"I'm so happy to see you." I smiled, and Baxter grinned back.

The living room felt better, now that Baxter was there. Because if his whapping tail and crazy bounding hadn't broken anything yet, maybe I wouldn't, either. The purple couch and the orange chair looked as comfortably mushy as our couch. The wooden floor gleamed in the sunlight streaming through the window, but the wood was old and scuffed, just like at our house. If Baxter

belongs here, I thought, I do, too.

I stood up. "Are you ready for a walk?"

Instead, he turned and looked back toward the doorway to the basement stairs.

And that's when I noticed a strange buzzing sound, and since the lab was down there, I thought, Well, it's probably not the washing machine.

At that moment, I realized that Professor Reese might be *home* and that I hadn't knocked on the door, I'd just let myself inside. But it seemed sort of silly to go back outside, lock the door, hide the key under the begonia, and go around to the front door to ring the doorbell.

The buzzing getting louder decided it for me. Baxter took off for the basement, and I followed him.

As I came down the stairs, I saw Professor Reese sitting in front of the main computer: all the cables came out the back like it was the head of a big octopus, connecting to the console, the other computers, and what used to be a tanning bed.

And what used to be a tanning bed was now vibrating, glowing with a red light.

"Professor Reese?"

She jerked in surprise and turned. "Jordie, you gave me such a fright!"

"I knocked on the front door, but I guess you didn't hear

it." (That wasn't technically true, but if I *had* knocked, she wouldn't have heard it over the buzzing, so it was sort of untechnically true.) "I came to walk Baxter. Like we talked about," I reminded her, in case she was mad I'd just come into her house, like a lot of grown-ups would be in a situation like this. Only I didn't think a lot of grown-ups would *be* in a situation like this—because what used to be a tanning bed had started vibrating like crazy.

I walked down the rest of the stairs. "What are you doing?" And I had to raise my voice because it was getting noisy.

"A system check," she said as the buzzing got even louder.

Baxter tucked his tail between his legs and scooted under one of the desks. The vibrating increased, and the buzzing got louder and louder until I practically had to yell, "Is it supposed to do that?"

"I have no idea!" she yelled back. "This is the first time I've ever tried it with all the components hooked up together!"

What used to be a tanning bed looked like it was going to vibrate itself into a pile of little pieces on the floor. The glowing got redder and redder. Professor Reese's eyes got wider and wider. The buzzing grew so loud the hairs stood up on the back of my neck.

All of a sudden there was a huge *POP*!

When the *POP* popped, three things happened at the same time: Professor Reese jumped back in her seat, Baxter bolted up and bonked his head on the underside of the desk, and I screamed (just a little).

My scream made Professor Reese scream, too, so all in all things were very exciting for a minute.

Then one of the little computers went *beep-beep-boop*, and Baxter whipped his head around and *boop*ed back. What used to be a tanning bed wasn't glowing or vibrating or buzzing anymore. It was just sitting there, still in one piece somehow.

I walked a little closer (but not *too* close). "What *is* this thing?"

"It's part of the project I'm working on—but I'm not ready to talk about it yet."

"Oh."

She walked over to the electronic console with lights and buttons, and pushed the big red one off.

She turned to me. "Let's take Baxter on a walk—I need to find my hat."

"Um . . . OK," I said, thinking if I had just made a basement full of equipment, an old lady, a girl, and a shaggy dog practically blow up, I wouldn't be wondering where my hat was. But maybe when you're a physicist, that's just a regular day at the office. "I have to get TJ first." I hurried up the stairs. "Be right back!"

I stuck the key back under the begonia and ran home.

TJ was at his desk, working on his stop-motion short. He moved Caveman's right leg a step forward.

He took a picture.

"Come on! It's time for Baxter's walk!"

"In a minute."

TJ moved Caveman's left leg a step forward.

He took another picture.

"If we don't go now, she'll leave without us!"

I hurried into the kitchen and came back out with three Popsicles. TJ grabbed the only cherry one, of course, which meant Professor Reese and I were stuck with grape.

Then we all set off to find Professor Reese's hat.

On the weekend, when we'd walked around the neighborhood, Baxter had stayed calmly at our sides. But now he charged ahead, pulling me down the street. I had to hold on to the leash with both hands, which meant TJ got to eat my Popsicle.

"He's galloping!" Professor Reese said.

"He's crazy!" TJ hurried behind me with a Popsicle stick in each fist.

"Is he heading to where you think you lost your hat?" I asked.

"As a matter of fact," Professor Reese huffed as we were

all practically running by then, "he *is*. Interesting."

We practically ran a few more blocks until suddenly Baxter reached an intersection and stopped. He looked around.

Professor Reese read the street sign. "Nineteenth Avenue." She studied Baxter for a moment. "Hmm." She started looking around, too. "Do either of you see my hat?"

All I saw were some apartment buildings, some trees, and a parking lot. "Your hat's red, right?"

But Baxter was taking off again, pulling me farther down the street.

"Where are you going?" TJ ran after me.

"Come back!" Professor Reese called. "It should be right here!"

"That's not what Baxter thinks!" The leash went up and down as he bounded ahead. We all just tried to keep up with him, TJ dropping plops of Popsicle slush as he ran.

When we reached the intersection, I looked across the street. There was the red hat, sitting on top of a newspaper stand.

"He found it!" I let Baxter pull me across the street.

He rose up on his hind feet and thwumped his front paws down on the newspaper stand, one paw on each side of the hat. His tail wagged a million times a minute.

Professor Reese puffed up to join us. "I thought we'd find it closer to Nineteenth."

TJ shrugged. "Maybe the wind blew it."

But there wasn't a breath of wind. Every leaf was still.

Professor Reese turned to Baxter and said, "How on earth did you do that?"

STUDY BUTT-IES

As we walked back to Professor Reese's house, I asked, "Have there been any calls from the flyers we put up about Baxter?"

"Nothing yet, dear," Professor Reese answered.

I thought, Yay! And I kept thinking it, the whole way home.

When we got there, Mom was just getting out of the car. It was a great opportunity to show her how dependable I was being.

"We just did Baxter's walk, right on schedule," I said.

"Great!" Mom smiled.

"Jordie and TJ were very helpful," Professor Reese said. Then she turned to me. "Can you walk Baxter again tomorrow?"

I looked at Mom and TJ, and they both nodded—Mom's nod meaning, *Yes*, and TJ's meaning, *Ha-ha, you have to do my chores again.*

"I can walk Baxter every day for the rest of my life!" I said.

The next morning, I ran to school to tell Megan all about dog walking Baxter. "Can you come over today to meet him?"

"No. My mom said she has to look at my schedule." Then she frowned. "She and Dad are mad at each other because the piano recital is on one of *his* weekends."

"Doesn't he want to come?" I asked as we walked toward the classroom.

"He does. But my grandma and grandpa just called last night and said they want to come, too. They're flying in just for the recital. And since they are my mom's parents, they always stay at Mom's, not Dad's." She sighed. "So now Dad is mad because Mom wants me to stay home and spend time with them and not go to Dad's at all that weekend."

"Can't they switch weekends?"

She shrugged. "Probably. If they change all the other stuff they already have planned. It's just always so complicated."

I gave her a quick hug. "I'm sorry."

"Thanks." She smiled.

But even if Megan couldn't come over right away, she'd be able to come over *sometime*. So all during math I tried to figure out—with Mrs. A. interrupting a million times— the fun things that me and Megan could do with Baxter that would cheer her up for sure. I couldn't wait until recess to tell her!

But right as Mrs. A. was dismissing everyone, she said, "Jordie and Tyler, could you come here for a minute?"

"I didn't do anything!" Tyler protested, which is what he always says right after he does something.

"You're not in trouble," Mrs. A. said. "You've been chosen for a special honor."

So me and Tyler went up to her desk to find out what it was.

"This week we're starting our Second-Grade Study Buddy program," Mrs. A. said. For the next two weeks, instead of morning recess, two fifth-grade Buddies would go help in a second-grade classroom. "I'd like you to be our class's first Buddies."

"Do I have to?" Tyler whined.

But I thought, She chose me first!

I knew exactly why I'd been chosen: my excellent people skills. She must have chosen me to balance out Tyler because he did not have excellent people skills, unless by "people skills" you mean making farting noises with your armpit or sticking girls' pencils up your nose (the eraser end, not the pointy end)—in which case, he was ready for the Nobel People Prize.

He complained up one hallway and down the other to the second-grade classrooms, but I couldn't wait to get to Room Six. When we came in, the little kids were all smiley. The bulletin board said *Welcome, Study Buddies* with *Jordie* and *Tyler* beneath. There was even juice and cheese and crackers for a Welcome Study Buddies Party.

My group was two girls: Maya, who peeked out at me from under her bangs, and Katie, who'd already finished her snack except for some crumbs stuck to her hands and chin, from where it looked like her juice box leaked.

They were so cute—they loved me right away.

My group was so excited to have a Study Buddy! Tyler's group was excited, too, because the first assignment was to measure things with centimeter rulers, and his two kids—a boy named Logan and a girl named Chloe—were already having a sword fight.

"Settle down," Mrs. Wilson said, but then she went back to teaching the rest of the class. Soon Tyler was sword fighting, too.

My group measured the length of a stapler (12 cm), the

height of a book (31 cm), and the width of the computer monitor (41 cm). We even measured the diameter of my crackers (4.25 cm) before I ate them, which wasn't part of the assignment. But Dad always says a little extra credit never hurt anyone, and I figured the decimal would look good in there.

I was having so much fun with Katie and Maya that I decided me and Megan's full-service salon should be a vet/beauty parlor/*day care*: when I gave the dogs a bath, the kids of the women getting their hair done could help scrub. It would be perfect because then their hands would be clean for lunch.

Tyler's group was having fun, too, but no one was measuring anything because they were so busy whapping one another's arms with the rulers. And right about the time I heard him say, "I didn't do anything!" I had a feeling that Tyler wasn't going to be a very good Study Buddy.

By the next morning, Tyler had changed "Study Buddies" to "Study Butt-ies." He made butt jokes up one hallway and down the other, like:

> *Tyler: Knock, knock.*
> *Me: Who's there?*
> *Tyler: U. R. A.*

Me: U. R. A. who?

Tyler: You are a butthead.

Tyler: What do you call a guy whose face looks like a butt?

Me:

Tyler: "Buttface," you butthead. What else would you call him?

Tyler: What did one butthead do when the other butt-head made a joke?

Me: Shut up, Tyler.

Tyler: Crack up. Get it?

By the time we got to Room Six, I'd decided that Tyler was the butthead and also that I'd have to remember that last joke to tell TJ because he'd like it.

When we went into Mrs. Wilson's room, Katie and Maya were sitting at the table with the goldfish aquarium.

"We've been talking this morning about how observations teach us about the world," Mrs. Wilson explained. Me and Tyler were each supposed to help our group write down five observations about the fish.

So Tyler sat down on one side of the table with Logan and Chloe, and I scooted in with Maya and Katie on the opposite side of the aquarium.

"OK, first we need to observe the fish," I said. Maya took turns peeking at the fish and then peeking at me. Katie just stuck her face up to the aquarium glass, her tongue working at a dried blob of something strawberry in the corner of her mouth.

"Now we need to write down what the fish look like," I said.

Katie sat back in her chair. "Their eyes are round."

"Good." I wrote it down. "What else?"

"They're orange," Katie added. "They wiggle their tails."

I wrote all that down. Then I turned to Maya, because she hadn't said anything yet. "What do you observe about the fish, Maya?"

Her eyes got big. She turned and looked at the fish, and me and Katie waited.

We waited some more.

It was hard to wait because Maya was *looking* at the fish, but I didn't know if that was the same thing as *observing* them and if that was supposed to take longer.

Katie bounced up and down in her chair. Her hair was tangly, and one of the tangles had a big strawberry blob that stuck out and bounced up and down, too.

Maya leaned forward, resting her chin on her hands on the tabletop. So I leaned down to look deep into the aquarium, too.

I could see Tyler's group through the glass, huddled around their paper. He wrote down their last observation, and they all laughed. Then Logan started sucking in his cheeks and puffing out his lips to make fishy lips.

I looked over at Maya. She sat back and brought her hands up by her shoulders and wiggled her fingers.

"They wiggle their arm fins?" I asked her.

She smiled and nodded.

I wrote it down. "Can you think of something you like to do that the fish like to do, too?" I was thinking she'd say "swim" or maybe "eat," and then we'd be done.

So Maya observed the fish some more. Katie jiggled her legs, and the hair blob jiggled right along, and I watched Tyler's group through the aquarium glass.

Logan stuck his fishy face right in front of Chloe. She pushed him away.

I heard the tiniest voice say, "They like to hide."

I turned and saw that Maya was pointing to one little fish hiding in the aquarium plants. "Good observation!" I wrote it down.

But then Chloe started making a fishy face, too. She and Logan pushed each other more. And just as Mrs. Wilson looked over and said, "Tyler!" Chloe pushed Logan so hard, she knocked him against the table. I barely had time to pick up our assignment before a slosh of water slopped

out of the aquarium onto the tabletop.

The whole class watched as Mrs. Wilson hurried over.

I held our paper out to her. "We're done with our assignment."

She nodded. "Good." But she didn't take it because she was too busy picking up Tyler's paper. She read it and frowned. Then she handed it to me. "Could you put them on my desk, please, Jordie? It's a *little wet* over here."

I said good-bye to Maya and Katie and carried the papers over. Tyler had written:

1. Fish are wet.
2. Fish don't talk.
3. Fish are boring pets.
4. Fish make bubbles from their mouth.
5. They make bubbles out the other end, too.

Mrs. Wilson said, "Jordie, could you tell Mrs. A. that Tyler will be late returning to class? We need to have a chat." And by the way she was glaring at Tyler, I had a feeling she thought he really *was* a Study Butt-y.

The rest of the day, I took sneaky looks at Tyler, once he got back to class, to see if he was upset about Mrs. Wilson's chat. But he didn't seem any different than before. And when me and TJ walked Baxter by the park after school,

Tyler was shooting hoops, same as always.

When we got back to Professor Reese's house, we found her in her lab, making notes in a notebook. TJ rolled around on the spinny chair. I snuggled Baxter on his bed (which Professor Reese had brought down to the lab) and told her about me and Tyler at Study Buddies. "I get why Mrs. A. chose *me*, but I can't believe she chose Tyler—he's like . . . I don't know, the worst kid in the whole class."

She looked up from her notebook. "Did Mrs. A. *say* that?"

"No." I shook my head. "She didn't need to say it *out loud*. Everybody just *knows*."

"Hmm. That's a pretty big assumption." Professor Reese turned back to her notebook.

And just as I snuggled into the warm fur on Baxter's fuzzy neck, she added, "You might want to think about that some more."

A REALLY GOOD HOME FOR BAXTER

When me and TJ got home from school the next day, I said, "Let's get Baxter!"

But TJ said, "I want a snack."

So after I paced around the kitchen, eating *my* string cheese and then pacing some more while TJ ate *his* string cheese (and then his *other* string cheese, his handful of crackers, his apple, and his bowl of cereal—seriously, I swear), we ran over there.

Professor Reese wasn't home from work yet, which meant I'd get another solo (if you didn't count TJ) walk with Baxter. I liked the solo walks best because then it really did feel like Baxter was half my dog.

We took off, Baxter sniffing everywhere. Everyone

wanted to pet him, even Tyler shooting hoops at the park. And I said yes because it's good to be generous with your dog.

As we left the park, I asked TJ, "Do you know Tyler?"

"Yeah, he's in Video Club. He's been helping me with my short. He's nice."

"Tyler's in Video Club? *That* Tyler right there?"

TJ looked at me like, *What's wrong with you?* "Yeah. That Tyler."

But I just shrugged because you could be nice and still be the worst kid in the whole class, couldn't you?

When we got back to Professor Reese's house, she was home from work. We found her in the lab, putting a big map of Portland up on her bulletin board.

She patted Baxter's head. "How was your walk?"

"Great!" I plopped down on Baxter's bed and thumped it to call him over. "Have there been any calls for Baxter?"

"Not yet."

"Well, I can keep walking him every day—no problem!" I said as he flopped down next to me.

"Good." She stuck a green pin in one spot on the map and a red pin in another.

TJ walked over to the map. "What are the pins for?"

"The green one shows where I thought I'd find my hat and the red one shows where Baxter actually found it."

She studied the map. "The question is, why wasn't the hat where I thought it would be?"

I lay down and rested my head on Baxter's tummy. "Maybe you forgot where you were walking when you lost it."

She frowned. "I don't think that's it."

When me and TJ got to the lab after school the next day, Professor Reese was still frowning. She stuck a new green pin in a new spot on the map. "Maybe we'll have better luck today," she said.

"You lost your hat *again*?" TJ said as we all followed Baxter up the stairs and out the door.

Baxter galloped, pulling me down the sidewalk, and Professor Reese and TJ practically ran behind us. When we reached the corner of Seventeenth and Lovejoy, Professor Reese nodded. "All right. My hat should be here—"

But Baxter pulled me three blocks farther, where he found it, like magic.

"You did it again!" Professor Reese said to Baxter.

He wagged his tail.

TJ grabbed the hat, and we turned toward home. And that's when I noticed a Baxter flyer on a streetlight pole, looking old and faded. I realized it was *Friday*, and it had been almost a whole *week*!

I thought, No one has called about Baxter!

The whole walk home, it was like a drum beating with every step: no one has called, no one has called, no one has called about Baxter.

No one had called saying they had a really good home. Now that I was dog walking, there was no reason why Professor Reese couldn't be the really good home. And actually, it was a really *great* home because I lived next door to it.

So as soon as we got back to the lab, TJ spun around in the spinny chair, and I decided it was time to convince Professor Reese. "So it's been almost a week, and no one has called about Baxter."

"That's true." She stuck a red pin in the spot where Baxter had just found the hat.

"I'll bet he's great company when you go to bed and when you wake up," I added.

"He is." She studied the map, tapping her fingers on her chin.

"He's great company while you're working in the lab, too."

Professor Reese turned to me. "Jordie, is there something you're trying to tell me?"

I took a deep breath. "Please let Baxter stay. You don't need to find him a really good home—he already *has* one. He has *us*."

She sighed. "I know you love him, Jordie. And you've been very helpful this week. But even when I'm home, I'm very busy with my work . . ."

"I can keep helping you! All I do in the afternoons is get stuck with TJ—"

"Hey!" he cried.

"And Baxter helps you, too," I added. "He helps you find your hat."

Professor Reese opened her mouth like she was going to say something, and then she closed it. She looked over at the map, then down at Baxter. "Hmm. Excellent point."

Baxter cocked his left eyebrow up at her.

She turned to me. "I'd need you to give him a walk every day after school."

"I will!" I nodded as hard as I could, and when I looked over, Baxter was nodding, too.

She studied his face for a moment. "All right."

And just like that, like it was no big deal (even though I was whooping inside!), Baxter was officially half my dog!

Professor Reese said, "We'll need some supplies. Want to go to the pet store?"

But I don't know why she even asked, because *of course.*

SPECTROMETERS AND ELBOWS

When we got back from the pet store, I ran home to tell Mom the great news—me and Professor Reese were keeping Baxter! "So I'll need to keep walking him every afternoon and maybe on the weekends, too," I said as she pulled stuff for dinner out of the fridge, "but I already said yes because I knew you'd think it was a great opportunity to be *really* dependable!"

Then I ran out of the kitchen before she could point out that I maybe should have checked with her first.

I grabbed the phone and took it into my room so I could call Megan and tell her, too.

"That's awesome, Jordie!" Megan said. "I can't wait to meet him!"

"You'll love him!" I said, and I got jumpy excited just thinking about it! "Oh, and I wanted to ask you something about our vet/beauty parlor. I think we should add a day care, too!" I told Megan how I'd started thinking about it when I was having so much fun with Maya and Katie. "And we know a lot of the women getting their hair done will be moms, so they can just bring their kids with them!"

"OK," Megan said. "I'll probably want to get a special salon cape for kids in case any of *them* need a haircut—they make really cute ones with animals on them. And maybe some special kids' shampoo . . ."

So it was all set. When I climbed into bed that night, between the vet/beauty parlor/*day care* news and the keeping-Baxter news, I could barely sleep.

In the morning (Saturday = Baxterday!), I brought my dog books into the kitchen to read while I ate my Crispy Rice. Now that I was officially half a dog owner, I had a lot to learn.

The books talked about how to help your new dog overcome the "insecurity" of a new home: You needed to give him a quiet place to retreat to (and Baxter had *two* beds now—his old bed and a new bed that I'd just chosen at the pet store). You also needed to spend lots of time with him so he wouldn't be lonely.

Baxter hadn't seen me all night. My half might be feeling lonely and insecure.

I ran over to Professor Reese's house. But when I got to the front door, I didn't know if it was too early to knock.

I didn't see anyone through the living room window. I went around to the side of her house and got down on my hands and knees to peek into the lab window.

There was Baxter, all adorable on his old fuzzy bed that I'd tucked under a desk. (We'd put the new pet store bed upstairs because I wanted the old bed to stay in the lab—I liked its Baxter smell.) And next to him was Professor Reese, sitting at a table lit by a bright lamp. She was looking into this piece of equipment that was like a microscope, only with two tube thingies sticking up instead of one.

I thought, Huh. What's that?

I knew Mom wouldn't let me hang out at Professor Reese's without TJ. I ran back home and into his room. "Wake up!" I hopped up to sit on the end of his bed, bouncing it hard when I landed. "Baxter might still be insecure! We need to get over there."

TJ groaned and pushed me off with his feet. "I need to work on my short today. I only have seventy-eight pictures."

"TJ, we have a deal!"

He opened his eyes and glared at me. "We have a deal for an afternoon walk—*one walk* for all my chores." He

rolled over to face the wall.

I slumped down on the bed again. I didn't want to see Baxter for only one little walk—I wanted to see him all weekend. Plus, I wanted to know what the weird microscope thingy was.

TJ would never want to go over just to see Baxter. But maybe I could convince him that hanging out in the lab was *Fun!* "Professor Reese has a new piece of equipment in her lab!" And I made it sound as *Fun!* as possible.

He rolled back over and opened his eyes. "What is it?"

"I don't know! I'm going to go find out!!" And I said that with an extra exclamation point. "Eat your breakfast and come on over!" Then I ran out again.

When I got back to the lab window, I knocked on it as politely as I could. Baxter woofed, and Professor Reese jumped in her chair. But then she motioned me in.

Baxter met me crazy happy at the back door. "Saturday is Baxterday!" I nodded, and he nodded, too. Then we went down to the lab so I could see what the new piece of equipment was. "What is that?"

"A spectrometer," Professor Reese answered. "It belongs to the science museum, but sometimes I borrow it for a day."

"What does it do?"

"Scientists use spectrometers in different ways. I'm using

this one to study different wavelengths of light." She smiled at me. "Want to see?"

When I looked through the "adjustable telescoping eyepiece," I saw the rainbow color band but with the red and indigo-violet ends shorter than the posters on the wall showed.

"Are you doing an experiment?" I asked.

"Not exactly," she said. "Right now I'm thinking."

"Oh. What are you thinking about?" I'd never thought while looking through a spectrometer before, and I wanted to try it.

"T-waves." Which, she told me, she had *discovered*, all by herself. Only she had discovered them so recently that *no other scientists* knew about them.

"Can I see one?" I asked. And even though I didn't know what a T-wave was, I started feeling excited because it wasn't even on the *posters* yet.

So I looked into the spectrometer again at the rainbow color band, and she explained, "What you're looking at is the middle section of the electromagnetic spectrum. Now imagine it's laid out flat, as if you had placed a ruler down on a table and were standing over it, looking down on it."

"OK," I said.

"Now I'm going to recalibrate the spectrometer"—and here she began adjusting the adjustable telescoping

71

eyepiece—"until it's as if you squatted down with your eye level to the top of the table and looked at the ruler from the side . . . just . . . like . . . so . . ."

The color band got narrower and narrower as the eyepiece rotated until I was looking at the color band sideways. It was so thin, even thinner than a ruler, that it almost disappeared completely. "I can barely see it anymore."

"Just wait . . ." she said.

All of a sudden, on the red end of the rainbow, there was a tiny flash of white light like a piece of glitter glinting in the sun. "Hey!"

"You've just seen a T-wave." She smiled.

I got up and walked over to study the posters on the walls. "What does it do?" Because if radio waves sent music and X-rays showed you skeletons and microwaves made popcorn, I was wondering what was left.

"I've been asking myself that question for months."

She sat back down at the spectrometer, and I tried to figure out what I could do so that Baxter would be half mine on the weekends, too. And the best thing I could think of was to help her as much as I could by making Baxter as happy as I could. "Can me and Baxter play in the yard with his new ball?" I asked because we'd bought one at the pet store and hadn't even opened it yet.

"I'm sure he'd enjoy that," she said.

So me and Baxter ran upstairs to the kitchen. The pet store bag was still on the counter. I found the ball—and actually the package called it a Superbouncy Ball, but since it was just sitting there in the shrink-wrap, how would you know?

I unwrapped it, and then we headed out to the yard. The ball *was* superbouncy, which was really fun because that made Baxter superbouncy, too. I threw it, and he followed the bounce, running after the ball and catching it in his mouth right after it had thwacked down on the ground and was coming back up.

TJ arrived, chewing a big wad of gum. I grabbed onto Baxter's collar since he was looking a little exuberant, and we all went down to the lab.

Professor Reese showed TJ a T-wave. Then he wandered over to spin in the spinny chair, and she sat back down in a boring chair to look into the spectrometer again.

Baxter trotted to his bed. I snuggled in next to him. When I looked up, Professor Reese was peering into the spectrometer again and thinking—hard, it seemed, because whenever I asked something, she was dreamy and quiet and didn't finish her sentences.

"Are you going to work in the lab all day?" I scritched Baxter's chin.

" . . . hmm? . . ."

I noodled Baxter's ears. "I could take him on all his walks today, if you want."

"Yes, well . . ." But then she was thinking again.

I patted Baxter's tummy and started thinking, too—only, instead of T-waves, I thought about Baxter.

Sometimes he was all bony, like he had a dozen elbows sticking out everywhere, and it took a second to find a place to cuddle up next to him. But as soon as he relaxed, all the elbows went away, and then he was a big fuzzy pillow. I rested my head against his belly and wondered how that was possible and if everybody was like that or just dogs.

Meanwhile, TJ had gotten up and was fidgeting around the lab, picking up stuff, even dumb stuff like a coffee mug full of pens, and putting it back.

Pretty soon, I started feeling sleepy. My head rose and fell as Baxter's breathing snuffled down his long nose and got quiet and full of sighs.

And then TJ said, "What are those numbers for?"

He was standing next to the map of Portland, pointing to a little slip of white paper stuck under one of the red pins (the where-Baxter-actually-found-the-hat pins). The map, I now saw, had a tiny slip of paper stuck under each pin, which I hadn't noticed when I'd walked in because I'd been so busy thinking about spectrometers and elbows.

But when TJ is fidgety, he notices stuff, even stuff Mom

doesn't want him to. Plus, he likes numbers in general, so he notices them even more. "45.533529, –122.689605," he read off one of the slips.

" . . . hmm?" Professor Reese looked up from the adjustable eyepiece. "Those are GPS coordinates." She turned back to the spectrometer.

"Oh." TJ wandered over to the bookcase to fidget some more.

But I thought, Wait a minute, what? Because I knew GPS coordinates showed you exactly where something was. Like, *exactly*. Like, *careful-we-have-to-land-this-rocket-ship* exactly, or *aaah!-the-asteroid-hurtling-toward-Earth-will-land-in-this-spot* exactly. Not *oops-lost-my-hat-around-here* somewhere.

"You wrote down the GPS coordinates for your hat?" I asked.

"What? . . . oh yes . . ." Professor Reese said and drifted back to the spectrometer.

I squeezed out from under the desk and sat up. "For your *hat*?" Baxter squeezed out from under the desk, too, and stood next to me, leaning against my shoulder. "Why would you do that?"

TJ wandered toward the back of the lab, running his hand along the electronic console and fingering the lights and buttons.

I wrapped my arms around Baxter's ribs. He rested his chin on the top of my head. "Why would it matter *exactly* where it was, as long as you found it again?"

"Hmm? . . ." Professor Reese said, refocusing the eyepiece. "Don't play with the teleporter, dear . . ."

TJ snatched his hands away from what used to be a tanning bed and shot me a look like, *Huh?*

"Wait." My head clunked on Baxter's chin as I scrambled to my feet. *"What did you just say?"*

Professor Reese's face popped up from behind the spectrometer. "Oh." Her eyes got big. "Uh . . . what did it sound like I said?"

"It sounded like, 'Don't play with the teleporter, dear.'"

"Oh my." She looked a little sick. "I didn't mean to say that, but apparently I did." She took a deep breath. "And now it looks as if I must ask you two a very important question: How good are you at keeping a secret?"

10

BAXTER AND THE *BOOP*

"**I**'m excellent," I told Professor Reese. "I'm the best secret keeper ever. Just ask anyone." Then I thought about it. "Well, don't ask anyone 'cause nobody ever believes I am. But really, I'm excellent—"

"What do you mean, *teleporter*?" TJ broke in. "That's *crazy!*"

"At first glance, it would appear so," Professor Reese agreed. "But it's true."

"A teleporter. *A teleporter.*" TJ's eyebrows climbed higher and higher up his forehead. "Like you stick something in and push a button and it ends up somewhere else? You mean *teleportation*?"

"I do." Professor Reese nodded.

TJ's jaw dropped so far his gum fell out of his mouth, and he had to catch it, quick. "A teleporter! Cool!"

Professor Reese grinned. "I know!"

"So T-waves are . . . ?" I asked.

"Teleportation waves," she said.

"And your hat wasn't really lost, was it?" TJ asked.

She shook her head. "I've teleported it. Twice."

TJ shrugged. "Don't worry. I'm not going to tell anyone." He stuck his gum back in his mouth. "They'd never believe it, anyway."

"Exactly," Professor Reese said. "And if you were a *little old lady* and told anyone, they wouldn't believe it *and* they'd probably think you were senile. And you'd lose your job at the university. And they'd ship you off to a nursing home."

"But why do you have to keep it a secret?" I asked. "If anyone doesn't believe you, you can just show them."

Professor Reese walked over to the map and touched the pins lightly. "There's still a big problem: the hat doesn't land where I think it will."

"So what?" I asked.

She turned to me. "The first thing the scientific community is going to demand is a demonstration. Then they'll ask why the landing site doesn't match the coordinates I put into the computer, and how it is that Baxter finds it so easily when I can't. I don't want to give a demonstration until I can answer those questions. I don't want to tell the world about T-waves until I have a better understanding of how they work."

"OK." I noodled Baxter's ears and stared at the pins on the map. "That makes sense. You want to figure it out first."

"Yes," Professor Reese said. "And so far I haven't had any luck."

"Well, we can help you," TJ said.

"Right," I added, "because Dad always says three heads are better than one." (Which I guess is true even if one of the heads is TJ's.) "So, let's teleport that hat again, and we can all try to figure it out together." I nodded, and when I looked over at Baxter, he was nodding, too—so actually that meant *four* heads.

"All right," Professor Reese said. "Come take a look."

She walked over and lifted the top of what used to be a tanning bed. "I invented the teleporter by studying, of all things, a microwave oven repair manual." She smiled. "I replaced the tanning lightbulbs so that when I bring the lid down, whatever is inside the teleporter is surrounded by metal rods.

"Electricity travels from the wall socket to this high-voltage transformer." She pointed to a little metal box at one end of the teleporter. "It increases the house voltage to

over twenty times its normal strength."

"Wow!" TJ said.

"This powerful voltage activates the magnetron tube." She pointed to a different metal box. "It converts the high voltage into electromagnetic T-wave energy. The T-waves bounce around inside the teleporter as they hit up against the metal rods—"

"So whatever's *inside* the teleporter—" TJ broke in.

"Gets surrounded by T-waves and teleported," Professor Reese concluded.

"Huh." I peered in to get a better look. "Those two little boxes do all that?"

"Easy as pie. Though I do expect to get a whopping electric bill this month . . ." She shrugged. "Oh well." She turned on power to the teleporter, the console, and all three computers. "Want to see it in action?"

I started feeling nervous, because, even though I hadn't known what I was looking at at the time, I'd already *seen* it in action: vibrating, popping, and screaming. I said yes anyway. TJ just nodded, because he didn't know any better.

Professor Reese pulled up a map of latitude-longitude lines for Portland on one of her "auxiliary" computers. "Where should we send the hat?"

I pointed to a spot a few blocks from her house.

"All right. First we need to see what the GPS coordinates

80

are for that spot." She moved her mouse and double-clicked. The coordinates appeared in a small box at the bottom of the screen.

She walked over to her main computer (the head of the octopus) and pulled up a new screen. "Let me just log in—" She typed in a secret password (that just looked like a row of asterisks to me). Another screen appeared that said *Destination Coordinates* over a little box that already had numbers in it.

"Those are the old coordinates from last time," Professor Reese said. She hit the delete key, and the box went blank. "All right. Read me the new numbers, TJ."

TJ leaned toward the auxiliary computer screen and read out, "45.534101, –122.697802," and Professor Reese typed them in and pressed enter.

The numbers almost matched the little slips of paper already on the map, I noticed. "Do they always start with 45 and –122?"

"For Portland, Oregon—yes." Professor Reese explained that there were 90 degrees latitude above the equator and 90 degrees below. For longitude, there were 180 degrees east or west of an imaginary line called the prime meridian, which ran from the North Pole to the South through Europe, Africa, and the Atlantic Ocean. For locations west of the prime meridian, the number was expressed as a negative.

"That's why you need so many numbers after the decimal point," she explained, "to pinpoint exact locations."

She nodded to TJ. "Let's get this party started." She walked over to the console and pushed the big red button.

All three computers and the electronic equipment and the teleporter started quietly buzzing, like we were standing under a tree that had a beehive way up in its branches. "Would you like to put the hat in the teleporter, TJ?" she asked.

"Yeah!" He picked up the hat from the bookcase, placed it on the metal rods, and then closed the lid with a loud click.

The teleporter lit up, the light glowing red through the red plastic cover. TJ jumped back.

Suddenly, the buzzing got louder, like now we'd climbed up the tree and were standing in the middle of the beehive.

"Right now, the teleporter is scanning the hat to identify its molecular pattern." Professor Reese raised her voice above the buzz.

"Once the scan is complete," she continued, "it sends this information to the auxiliary computer."

At that moment, one of the smaller computers started blinking and whirring. And maybe the half of Baxter that belonged to Professor Reese the physicist wasn't scared, but my half was, so he tucked his tail between his legs and went to hide on his bed under the desk.

"The auxiliary computer stores the information," Professor Reese said. "This will be the instructions for putting the object back together."

"Back together?" TJ said.

"Once the information is stored, the auxiliary computer sends a signal to the other auxiliary computer"—and here the other little computer began to blink and whir—"which activates the equipment to commence T-wave generation . . . which should be . . ." She looked at her watch. "Right . . . about . . . *now.*"

The teleporter shuddered. TJ backed away even more.

"Once sufficient T-waves have been generated, the object inside the teleporter begins to break down to the molecular level."

"Break down?" TJ said.

The teleporter began to vibrate, and pretty soon it was rattling, and the reddish light grew stronger, the buzzing grew louder, like we were still standing in the beehive, only now the bees were mad about it.

I turned to TJ. "Don't worry—it only *looks* like it's going to explode!"

The red light got brighter and brighter. The buzzing got so loud, the hairs on the back of my neck stood up. Professor Reese raised her voice to a shout. "When the T-wave energy reaches capacity level, the object is teleported—"

And at that moment was the huge *POP!* (But this time I was expecting it, so only TJ screamed.)

Then everything got quiet, except for one cheerful *beep-beep-boop* that the first auxiliary computer made as it powered down, which made Baxter make a little cheerful *boop*ing noise of his own.

"It just sent the reconfiguration instructions via radio waves," Professor Reese said, pushing off the big red button. "And now that they've received the instructions, the hat molecules are reconfiguring back into a hat."

I ran over to the teleporter as TJ lifted the lid. "Wow!" he said.

Professor Reese wasn't crazy. It was like the teleporter had picked up the hat and put it down somewhere else.

That hat was *gone*.

We took the stairs two at a time. I grabbed the leash, and then we followed Baxter, his ears flapping as he galloped down the sidewalk.

When we got to the spot on Raleigh Street where the hat was supposed to land, Professor Reese barely had time to say, "This is the landing site . . ." before Baxter pulled me forward.

TJ raced beside us. At the corner, Baxter veered onto Twenty-Second, toward something red lying on top of a bush.

TJ yelled, "There it is! I see it!" and ran faster, but Baxter still beat him by a nose (which, considering how big Baxter's is, didn't surprise me). He'd found the hat again. Like magic.

"It works! It works!" TJ screamed. "The tele—"

I clamped my hand over his mouth and kept it there until Professor Reese caught up to us, huffing.

When I pulled my hand away, TJ was grinning. He strutted around like a football player doing a touchdown dance. He plucked the hat off the bush. Then he pulled it down on his head and whispered, *The teleporter works!*

THE SECRET LAYER
OF SCIENCE

The next morning, Professor Reese opened her door wearing a pink leotard and pink footless tights. She looked like a cupcake or maybe a piece of bubble gum. "I need a ten-letter word for 'strange and unconventional.'"

I thought, She probably knows a lot of those.

"It starts with *out* . . ." she continued, "but *outlandish* didn't work."

"Out of this world?" I said.

"Out of your mind?" TJ said.

"Out . . . of course!" she cried, writing *outrageous* in 16-across.

"Are we doing any teleporting this morning?" TJ asked.

Professor Reese shook her head. "I need to return the

86

spectrometer to the science museum before they open. Want to come along?"

Me and TJ ran home to check with Mom, who said yes. Then we ran over to Dad's.

"How about instead of waffles we connect when you get back?" he suggested. "I'll wait to take my lunch break at work until you call."

"Deal!" I said.

Me and TJ ran back to Professor Reese's. I gave Baxter a big kiss between his crazy eyebrows, and his kiss back landed on my chin. "We'll be home soon," I told him.

Then me and TJ and Professor Reese rode the streetcar to the museum, the spectrometer, in a little black case, sitting on her lap.

The science museum was on the banks of the Willamette River, tucked up beneath a huge bridge. But in spite of the roar of traffic above us, being by the river was nice. People biked and jogged down the riverfront path. Geese paddled around in the water.

We walked up to the front doors, but no one was there yet to let us in. "Let's go around to the employee entrance," Professor Reese said.

She led us around to a side door that had a keypad instead of a lock.

"Cool!" TJ crowded in. "Can I do it?"

"We're not supposed to share the code with anyone." But when she punched it in, TJ said, "Blast off!" which meant he'd seen it anyway. So Professor Reese let TJ try it.

"6-5-4-3-2-1 blast off!" he said as he punched in the numbers.

The door opened into the Turbine Hall, which was so tall, there was an airplane hanging from the ceiling. We walked past displays on solar technology and bridge building, and TJ ran his hands across everything, saying, "Cool!"

"My office is on the second floor, but the spectrometer belongs in here," Professor Reese said as we walked into the Physics Lab. "Could you get the lights, Jordie?"

I found the light switch and turned the lights on.

TJ ran over to where a sign said *Van de Graaff Generator*. It was a huge metal ball with a little handwheel attached. When you cranked it, Professor Reese explained, it rotated a belt that rubbed against a brush inside the ball. "Turning the crank charges the ball with static electricity, like when you shuffle across a rug in your stocking feet."

"Zap me!" TJ said.

So I cranked the handwheel, and TJ touched the huge ball and got zapped. He had me zap him (twice), and he yelled (both times).

"Do it again!" TJ said.

But I wanted to look at the displays. So while Professor

Reese electrocuted TJ, I wandered around the lab.

There were all kinds of technology, some of it really old: a microscope from 1929, a steam engine from 1890, and even some lightbulbs Thomas Edison designed in 1879. "They had lightbulbs back in 1879?" I asked.

"Indeed," Professor Reese answered.

"Huh," I said. I walked back over to the light switch and turned the lights off and then back on. Professor Reese looked over and smiled at me. I smiled back.

Before a week ago, I'd barely ever been in a science lab, and now I was in them all the time. But it was more than that. There was this secret layer of science that had always been there, when I made hot chocolate in Dad's microwave or turned on the lights. The secret layer of science was everywhere. I'd just never noticed it before.

Before Professor Reese.

I didn't always understand what she was talking about, but I liked it. Even the parts I didn't understand.

"I need to pick up something in the Life Science Hall," Professor Reese said. "Some*one*, actually." She turned to TJ. "And I think this will interest you in particular." She led us into the lobby and up the main stairs.

The Life Science Hall had a model of an ear so big you could crawl down the canal. There were displays on how muscles moved and how your brain worked. But Professor

Reese walked straight back to where the animals were: two kinds of slithery snakes, a red-kneed tarantula creeping across its tank, slimy bullfrogs squirming on rocks, and stick insects wobble walking along a branch.

TJ hurried ahead, saying, "I love this place!"

But I didn't, and that was because everything in the glass aquariums was creeping or squirming or slithering. I hung out by the tortoises because they barely moved.

I thought, Me and Megan's vet/beauty parlor/day care should only be for animals with fur. Anyone with a sick boa constrictor will just have to take it somewhere else.

"You said you had to pick up something?" I asked Professor Reese because, by then, all the creeping and squirming and slithering was making my skin crawl so much, they could have put me in one of the aquariums.

"Indeed." She walked into a back office and came out holding a clear plastic tank. "Come look," she called to TJ as she carried it over to me.

There wasn't any water in the tank. Instead, there was a layer of wood shavings, a curved-over piece of bark the size of a slice of bread, and a fat branch with twigs poking up. Three tiny white dishes held dry dog food, an orange slice, and a soggy sponge. On top of the whole tank was a clear plastic lid with air holes in it. "So, what do you think?" Professor Reese asked.

Me and TJ leaned in to look closer.

All of a sudden, two long skinny brown antennas waved out from underneath the curved bark . . . followed by a hard, shiny brown bug head . . . and then six spiky bug legs sticking out from a bug body . . . and then an abdomen that just kept coming and coming, sliding out in segment after segment of hard, shiny brown bug body.

"This is my Madagascar hissing cockroach," Professor Reese said. "I asked the museum to order an extra one for me."

"You paid money for that?" I asked.

But TJ was already saying, "Can I hold it?"

"You may when we get home." Professor Reese handed him the tank. "And you can carry the tank while we're on the streetcar."

So the whole way home, TJ held the tank on his lap, looking down through the lid at the big brown bug with its shiny bug head and its waving bug antennas and its long, gross bug abdomen (full of bug guts—you could just tell) and its six spiky bug legs. By the time we got off the streetcar, TJ was calling it "Spike."

He helped Professor Reese clear a space on the bookcase, while I cuddled Baxter. "You're not gross like a bug," I whispered as I shook my head. He shook his head back.

"TJ, why don't you go up to the refrigerator and find a

snack for Spike," Professor Reese said. "See what's in the vegetable drawer."

So TJ ran upstairs and came back down with a carrot. "I got a long skinny one so he can eat one end and walk up and down on the rest of it."

Professor Reese took the lid off the tank. When she picked up Spike, he started hissing and kicking out with his gross bug legs until she put him on TJ's hand.

Spike sat, waving his little bug antennas for a while. TJ just laughed.

Finally, Professor Reese said, "Let's give him the carrot and then get to work."

So TJ put Spike into the tank, stuck in the carrot, and put the lid back on while Professor Reese studied the map, and I scritched Baxter's ribs.

"We need to figure out how Baxter finds the hat when we can't. He must be using one of his five senses," Professor Reese said. "He can't taste or touch the hat until he finds it. And hats don't make any noise. Sight, perhaps?"

"But once you teleport the hat, he doesn't see it again until he finds it," I said.

"Good point." Professor Reese nodded.

TJ plunked down in the spinny chair. "Maybe the hat smells like us."

"Like those movies where a bloodhound follows criminals

through the woods," I added. We talked about what criminals always do, which is to run through a stream to wash
the scent off their feet (though that doesn't work so much
with TJ).

We decided to try that. We washed the hat in the washing machine (conveniently located in the lab). Then I ran
upstairs to get a plastic bag that I could wear like a glove to
pick up the hat and stick it in the dryer (also conveniently
located in the lab).

After the hat was dry, I used the plastic bag again to put
it in the teleporter (conveniently located near the washer
and dryer). Then we teleported the hat and followed Baxter to the destination site, where he barely stopped before
galloping on. But even though the hat didn't smell like us
anymore, Baxter found it, like magic.

Back in the lab, I put the hat on the bookcase. TJ read
out the coordinates while I wrote up the little slips of paper
and stuck them up—a green pin for the destination coordinates and a red pin for where the hat actually landed.

Professor Reese groaned as she studied the map. "There's
no *pattern*. The hat lands too far north. Too far west . . ."

"Too far southeast," TJ added helpfully, but I glared at
him to shut up.

"If there's no pattern, we can't predict where the hat will
land." She paced the lab. "We can't draw any *conclusions* if

every result is random."

"Maybe Baxter finds the hat because he's magical." That was the conclusion I'd drawn, because he could find the hat when we couldn't. Plus, he understood me perfectly. Plus, if there could be teleportation in the world, then why not a magical dog?

But Professor Reese just shook her head. "I'm a *scientist*, Jordie. I don't believe in magic." Then she plopped down in her chair and closed her eyes.

About this time, I thought that maybe Professor Reese might want "five minutes of peace and quiet," which is what Mom calls it, only she usually wants more than five minutes' worth. So I said, "Can me and TJ take Baxter to the park?"

Professor Reese nodded.

We ran upstairs. I used the phone in the kitchen to call Dad at work and tell him to meet us at the dog park.

"You want sandwiches?" he asked.

"Yeah!" I said. "See you there!"

I hung up the phone and grabbed the superbouncy ball from the kitchen counter. We followed Baxter as he trotted down the sidewalk, and for the first time, TJ held the leash. He was so happy, he made everyone else happy just by walking by (Baxter, certainly not TJ), which is the best kind of dog to have.

When we got to the park, we walked around letting Baxter sniff wherever he wanted, as long as he wanted. Pretty soon Dad was there with three sandwiches that were so big, they might as well have been four. But that was good because there were four of us. We all took turns taking a bite of a sandwich and then breaking off a piece to feed Baxter.

The whole time we ate, TJ told Dad about Spike. "When he crawls on your hand, you can feel his spikes on your skin!"

I shuddered.

"It's awesome!" TJ said.

"A dog and a cockroach." Dad laughed. "Professor Reese is going to be an interesting neighbor."

"I know!" TJ said.

"Especially because of Baxter!" I said. I held up the superbouncy ball. "Watch this!" I threw the ball superhard and made it bounce superhigh. But even though the ball superbounced all the way across the park, Baxter was able to track every bounce.

"Wow!" Dad said.

Soon, he was trying it. And when the other dogs at the dog park joined in—two little barky black ones and one with the cutest freckles on his nose—Baxter followed the bounce way better than they did and always got the ball

first. "Baxter has some serious ball-handling skills!" Dad said.

"Yep," TJ agreed.

"He's King of the Bounce!" I said.

It seemed pretty magical to me.

After a while, Dad checked his watch and said, "I need to get back to the store." So he took off.

TJ said, "I have to go work on my short now. I only have ninety-two pictures. That's only eleven point five seconds." And he took off, too.

So I took Baxter back to Professor Reese's by myself.

Professor Reese was by the kitchen door, watering the potted pink begonia. "How was the park?"

"Great!"

I unclipped Baxter's leash. He flopped down in the cool grass.

I wanted to flop down next to him, but I'd been gone from home so long, I figured I'd better go find a great opportunity to help Mom with something. If TJ was home and I wasn't, she'd notice.

I went in to the kitchen to put the ball and leash away and then came back out. "I have to go home now."

"Thank you for your help, Jordie."

"Sure!" I gave Baxter a big kiss on his nose, and his kiss back landed perfectly and only a little bit slobbery right on the tip of my chin. "Me and TJ will come over again tomorrow after school."

"Good." She smiled. "Because I'm counting on my lab assistants to help me."

And that night, climbing into bed, I realized—by "lab assistants" she meant TJ and me.

12

THE BAXTER STATION

When I got to school on Monday, Megan ran up to me on the playground. "Guess what? My mom said I can come over after school today!"

"Yay!" I was so excited I almost hopped. "I can't wait for you to meet Baxter—he's so much fun to cuddle, and his fur is so swirly and soft! You'll love him!" We started running to the bars. "Oh, and guess what? Professor Reese said I can be her lab assistant!"

"Cool!" Megan said.

When we got to the bars, Megan plopped down her backpack. "So I read an article about cutting kids' hair." She climbed up next to Aisha to balance on the bar. "I guess some kids are scared of the shampoo part, so the article said to just use a spray bottle with water to get their hair wet."

"You cut kids' hair?" Aisha asked.

"Not yet," Megan said. "But one day."

Me and Megan told her and Jasmine all about the vet/beauty parlor/day care, while Jasmine passed around a bag of oatmeal breakfast bars that she and her mom had baked the day before. When we were finished, Aisha said, "That sounds like so much fun! Can I work there?"

"Sure!" Megan said.

"I want to work there, too!" Jasmine said. "I can bake all the treats for the kids for snack time."

"Deal!" I popped the last bite of my breakfast bar into my mouth. Then I asked Aisha, "Do you want to work in the vet part or the beauty parlor part or the day care part?"

"Um . . ." She hopped down from the bar. "Could I do art lessons for the kids?"

"That's a great idea!" I said, and I felt a little relieved because it looked like no one wanted to do the vet part but me, which meant that even with four of us, I'd still get to do all the animal stuff.

Then the bell rang, and we all had to run to class. Mrs. A. was starting a language arts lesson on how to punctuate compound sentences, so I hurried to tell one last thing to Jasmine and Aisha—

"Jordie."

About how me and TJ were now lab assistants—

"*Jordie . . .*"

"Shhh!" Jasmine hissed. She snuck a peek at Mrs. A.

I thought, Exactly. If Mrs. A. would be quiet for a second, I could finish telling them about looking into the spectrometer. So I leaned in closer to whisper while Mrs. A. went on and on—

"JORDIE."

—about the stupid comma in sentence number three.

Mrs. A. was in an impatient mood, which made me wonder how come *kids* were the ones who got report cards with Needs Improvement on them (which of course I got because, as Dad always says, who *doesn't* need to improve on stuff? Nobody, that's who). But even though kids got report cards, *teachers* never did or maybe there would have been a Needs Improvement mark in the Patience column of Mrs. A.'s. Not that anyone ever asks me.

She was impatient all morning. I was so happy when it was finally time to leave for Study Buddies.

When me and Tyler got to Room Six, we walked over to the little table. Maya and Katie were sitting on one side, and Chloe and Logan were on the other side.

Tyler gave them high fives, while Maya peeked out from under her bangs to give me a smile, and Katie jumped up to hug me. Whatever she'd had for snack was stuck all over. After she hugged me, the sticky was stuck on my arms, too.

Me and Tyler sat down.

On each side of the table was a worksheet, a small, empty box, and two bags—one filled with little marbles and one filled with big marbles.

Mrs. Wilson came over to explain the assignment: our kids were supposed to predict if it would take more little marbles or more big marbles to fill up the empty box. Then we were supposed to see if we were right by filling the box first with little marbles and then again with big ones, counting how many marbles it took each time.

The answer was so obvious that I was surprised by the assignment—of course it would take more little marbles than big marbles to fill up the same space. But Mrs. Wilson said the purpose of the assignment was to start thinking like scientists, predicting what we thought would happen and then experimenting to find out.

We were supposed to write up our report on the worksheet. We had to fill out a section for WE PREDICT, WE DISCOVERED, and WE CONCLUDE.

Mrs. Wilson finished explaining and went back to working with the class, leaving me with my group, Tyler with his group—and a whole bunch of marbles.

My group got busy deciding what to write.

But it wasn't hard to PREDICT what would happen when Tyler and Logan and Chloe got busy: within a few

minutes their bag of little marbles tipped over. All the marbles rolled across the tabletop and clattered to the floor.

We DISCOVERED that it only takes Mrs. Wilson a few seconds to get from her chair across the room to the table where we were sitting. It didn't take a genius to CONCLUDE that Tyler was in trouble. Again.

But even though Tyler wasn't having a good day, I was having a great one, and that was because Megan was finally coming over after school to meet Baxter!

We blabbed the whole way home, with TJ tagging behind.

We dumped our backpacks in the living room. "Let's go get Baxter!" I said.

But TJ said, "I want a snack." He got out the crackers and the butter and started making his cracker stack—he makes a billion little cracker-butter sandwiches and stacks them on top of each other until it's a cracker tower. Then he demolishes it like he's Godzilla or King Kong or something. (There are crumbs everywhere, I swear.)

I grabbed two string cheeses, which me and Megan ate in ten seconds. We hurried TJ while he stacked up his crackers and hurried him even louder while he ate them.

When he was finally done, he grabbed a carrot from the refrigerator.

"Since when do you eat carrots for snack?" I asked.

"It's for Spike."

We all ran over to Professor Reese's. Baxter was waiting as we opened the door, his tail wagging so hard he practically fell over.

TJ ran past him and down the stairs to see Spike, but Megan stayed with me, petting and patting Baxter, his nose cool and wet against our hands.

"Aw!" she cried. "He's so cute!"

I was so happy that she thought Baxter was cute (though of course she would because everybody did). Megan scritched his neck and under his chin as Baxter wagged his tail. But then she looked up and said, "So what are we supposed to do now?"

And the way she said it made me suddenly wonder if, now that she'd met Baxter and petted him, he wasn't exciting to her anymore. What if she thought taking Baxter for a walk was a chore, like clearing the table or loading the dishwasher—the thing you *had* to do before you got to do the fun stuff?

It had taken forever to convince TJ that Baxter was *Fun!* but it had never occurred to me that I'd have to convince Megan, too.

"I got to choose his nice new collar at the pet store because his old collar was gross," I told her. "Doesn't the purple look pretty next to his silvery fur?"

"That's a great color on him," Megan agreed.

"I got to choose all the other stuff we got, too." I showed her the pile, still in the pet store bag on the kitchen counter.

"Oh!" Megan twisted the cap to the shampoo bottle and sniffed. "It smells nice." She picked up the dog brush and felt the bristles. "It kind of looks like the stuff I'll have at the beauty station of our vet/beauty parlor/day care!" She turned to me and smiled. "Let's set it up!"

"Great idea!" I said. "And instead of a beauty station, we can call it a Baxter Station!"

There was a little empty table by the back door. Megan picked up the dog shampoo and the brush, and I grabbed everything else, and we laid it all out on the little table.

Megan turned to Baxter. "Now let's fix you up." She brushed his neck and his back and even the fuzzy hairs on his long legs and then put the brush down. Then I picked it up and carefully brushed all the sticking-out hairs of his beard and sideburns and eyebrows.

I could have brushed Baxter all day—making the swirls of his grays and silvers even swirlier and the crazy parts sticking out on his face even crazier. But when I handed the brush back to Megan, she just put it on the Baxter Station like she thought he was swirly and crazy enough.

That made me worry because if Megan wasn't here with me, she'd probably be doing something fancy like piano or ballet or horseback riding.

I thought, What if hanging out with Baxter isn't enough?

She picked up the packet of dog treats. "Can we give him a treat?"

"Sure!"

So she gave him a treat, and then I gave him one, and he wagged his tail after both of them.

I picked up the superbouncy ball. "I taught him how to play ball. Do you want to go over to the dog park? I can show you."

So we yelled for TJ, who came running up the stairs, and we all headed over to the park.

Every time we threw the ball, it superbounced superfast, and so did Baxter. And even though there was a yellow Lab who tried to get the ball, Baxter always got it first.

"He's really good," Megan said.

"He's King of the Bounce!" I agreed.

I was happy because it looked like Megan was having *Fun!*

Then her cell phone rang. She answered, "Hi, Mom . . . OK." She shut her phone. "My mom's coming in a minute. We have to go back to your house so I can get my backpack."

So we ran home to our front yard. Right as TJ went inside to work on his short, my mom drove up and got out of her car.

Me and Megan told her all the things we'd done with Baxter. "We threw the superbouncy ball at the park!" I said.

"And we set up the Baxter Station!" Megan added, and then we told her how we organized it.

"Great!" Mom said. Then she smiled at Megan. "Do you want to stay for dinner, honey?"

"I can't. My mom's coming in a minute."

"Oh well," Mom said. "Next time."

"I'll wait here with Baxter while you get your backpack," I told Megan. "He can't come inside the house."

So they went inside, and I sat down in the grass, Baxter plunking down next to me.

The whole time Megan was gone, I worried if she'd had enough *Fun!* that she'd love hanging out with Baxter as much as I did.

But right as she came back out, I suddenly realized what I needed to do. I stood up, and Baxter scrambled to his feet.

"I need to show you one more thing," I told Megan. "Come stand right here in front of Baxter."

So she came over.

I reached over and tapped the top of her shoulder. "Up, Baxter," I said.

He reared up on his hind legs and planted his front paws on Megan's shoulders, so fast and heavy it practically knocked her over. "Wow, he's strong," she said.

They stood eye to eye, with his crazy silver eyebrows standing straight up and his black lips open, panting dog breath. "If you stand eye to eye with Baxter, then he understands what you are saying," I told her. "You just ask him something and then nod."

I walked around to stand behind her, so he could see eye to eye with me, too. "You want Megan to come over again, don't you, Baxter?"

I nodded, and he nodded back.

"You do?" she asked. Then she nodded.

I held my breath—because I'd never tried it with anyone else before, and I didn't know if it would work.

Baxter looked into my eyes. He looked back at Megan, who was still nodding.

He nodded, too.

"Yay!" Megan cheered. "I love him!"

He dropped back to the ground, and she gave him a big hug.

"So you want to come over again tomorrow?" I asked.

She sighed. "I don't think I can. I have lessons all week. Then my grandparents fly in on Friday morning, and I'm staying home from school to spend time with them—my mom and dad worked out the schedule." She rolled her eyes. "The recital is on Saturday."

"Oh. Are you excited?"

She shrugged. "Sort of." Then her mom drove up. "I wish I didn't have to go."

She climbed into the car and gave me and Baxter a little wave through the car window. She was still hugging her backpack to her chest as they drove away.

13

SPIKE TAKES A HIKE

When me and TJ got to the lab the next afternoon, we found Professor Reese on her hands and knees, crawling around the lab. "Watch where you step," she called out. "Spike is missing!"

"He's not in his tank?" TJ said.

"When I came down to feed him this afternoon, I discovered that the lid was off."

TJ's eyes widened. "I must have forgotten to put the lid back on yesterday after I gave him his carrot! I'm sorry!"

Professor Reese sat back on her heels. "It's not your fault, TJ. I didn't check on him last night, and he's my pet." She looked around the lab. "I know cockroaches are good climbers. He could be anywhere."

TJ dropped to his hands and knees and started crawling around the floor, too, looking under furniture. I checked the tops of all the desks, behind all the computer monitors, and underneath each keyboard. And Baxter sniffed everywhere.

"Be careful as you move things around," Professor Reese said as she slid the books off the bottom shelf of the bookshelf, handful by handful, to check behind them. "Cockroaches can fit into very small spaces."

I knelt down by Baxter. "We need to find Spike, OK?"

I nodded, and he nodded back.

I started peeking under the small cracks beneath things and between things, and Baxter stuck his nose next to mine. But even though he was magical about finding hats, he wasn't as magical when it came to cockroaches, so we all just crawled around.

"Let's take a break for a minute and think this through." Professor Reese stood and leaned up against a desk to rest. "I'm guessing he's still in the lab. Maybe instead of trying to find him, we could coax *him* to come to *us*."

"Here, Spike! Here, Spikey Spikey Spikey!" TJ called. "Come here, boy!"

Professor Reese smiled. "I don't think we can call him like we call Baxter. But we could put out some apple slices. I think he'll come looking for something to eat."

"Yeah, he's probably hungry by now!" TJ said.

So me and TJ ran upstairs and cut an apple into slices and put them on a bunch of little plates. We carried the plates downstairs and stuck them all over the lab.

"How about we get to work," Professor Reese said. "I bet Spike will be eating an apple slice by the time we get back."

"OK!" TJ looked happier.

"Good!" Professor Reese's eyes got all sparkly. "I thought up a different approach to our experiment that I want to try."

"Yay!" I said, and I wondered if maybe when you are a scientist, starting a new experiment feels like your birthday right before you get to open your presents.

Professor Reese's eyes kept sparkling as she explained her plan:

At exactly 3:00 p.m., me and TJ would teleport the hat, and Professor Reese would be waiting at the spot where the hat was *supposed* to land. She wanted to see if she could see, taste, hear, touch, or smell anything that would help her figure out how Baxter always knew where the hat actually *did* land. "It's a good thing I have lab assistants," she said. "I wouldn't be able to do this on my own." Which meant we really were helping her—she wasn't just pretending like some grown-ups do when they say *what a big help you were*, but you know you really weren't.

Me and TJ were doing *science*.

We looked at the map and chose a spot to send the hat. Professor Reese deleted the old coordinates on the main computer, and TJ read out the new ones for her to type in. "45.530313, –122.696471." Professor Reese left to walk to the landing site, and me and TJ and Baxter sat in the lab, waiting for three o'clock.

But the closer it got to three o'clock, the louder the clock on the wall ticked. Pretty soon, me and TJ couldn't talk anymore over the *tick-tick-tick*, and I started thinking that being a lab assistant was maybe not so great after all.

Because even though by then we'd seen a bunch of tele-portations, it was still scary to think about clicking down the lid of the teleporter and having the whole room start buzzing, angry-bee style. Even though it hadn't blown up before, what if for the first time it did?

At 2:59, I said to TJ, "So if you want to put the hat in, go ahead," like it was a really hot day and I was generously handing him the last Popsicle in the box. He said, "That's OK, you can do it," like he was pushing the Popsicle box right back at me. But by then it was 3:00, and we didn't have time to argue about it. So I grabbed his shirt and pulled him up out of the chair, and we got the hat off the bookcase and stuck it in the teleporter. Then we clicked the lid down together, so we'd blow up together.

Everything started buzzing and shaking, and it all

seemed even louder with Professor Reese not there. And when the *POP* popped, I screamed a little bit, even though I knew it was coming.

But we didn't blow up. After the last computer powered down with a final *beep-beep-boop* and Baxter *boop*ed back, I pushed off the big red button, and we headed out.

Even though we'd just teleported the hat, for once Baxter wasn't really galloping. He stopped between gallops to look around. Sometimes he shook his head or stopped to scratch his ear with his hind leg. Then he looked around some more.

I figured Professor Reese's half of Baxter must be looking for Professor Reese (even though my half was fine) and wondering where she was. I knew dogs loved their owners best of all because I'd been reading about dogs ever since me and Megan started planning our vet/beauty parlor, and I'd been reading even more about dogs since Baxter.

Me and TJ followed Baxter, who was sort of galloping all the way over to where we'd tried to send the hat.

Professor Reese was sitting on the curb. "Nothing," she said, but she didn't seem sad about it. "All right. That's good information to have—I'll have to think about that."

"How can you think about nothing?" I asked because when nothing happens that means nothing happened.

"Ah—but it's *not* nothing." She stood and smiled.

"Huh?" TJ said.

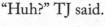

"The fact that I couldn't see or hear anything is new information. I need to see how it fits in with what I already know."

"So when you're a scientist, nothing is something?" I asked.

"Exactly."

When Baxter found the hat lying on a hedge two blocks south, Professor Reese just nodded. "We need to think this through some more."

TJ picked up the hat and plunked it down on his head.

And that's when I saw something slip down from beneath the edge of the hat, by TJ's left eyebrow: the hard brown tip of a gross bug abdomen. "Eww. There must have been a bug on this hedge because it's in the hat."

"Ahhh!" TJ whipped off the hat and flipped it over.

A big brown bug rolled down into the middle of the hat and landed on its back with its little feet in the air—not moving at all.

TJ's eyes got big. "Spike?"

"Oh my!" Professor Reese said.

"Uh-oh," I said.

"No!" TJ cried.

Because if Spike was in the *hat*, that meant that Spike had just been *teleported*—and we didn't know if he was OK or not.

14

CAVEMAN VS. ZOMBIE CHEERLEADER

"Spike? Are you OK?" asked TJ, and we all, even Baxter, leaned in to get a better look at Spike lying on his back, inside the hat.

"I've never teleported anything alive before," Professor Reese said quietly. "I don't know if the reconfiguration instructions can put a living being back together."

Spike *looked* the same. His little bug antennas still stuck out from the sides of his hard brown head. He still had six spiky bug legs and his long bug abdomen. But his bug antennas weren't wiggling, and the spiky legs weren't kicking.

Professor Reese shook her head. "I don't know if the instructions were detailed enough to restart his respiratory and circulatory systems."

Which meant she didn't know if Spike's little bug heart would ever beat again.

"Spike?" TJ tried once more. But Spike lay still.

"I'm so sorry, TJ." Professor Reese put her hand on his arm. "If it's any consolation, I don't think he felt anything."

And that's when I thought I saw an antenna twitch. "Wait!"

We all leaned in closer. Baxter started panting. "Come on, buddy!" TJ said.

And then there was a kick. And another. And another. And then all six spiky little legs were kicking like crazy as Spike tried to get right side up again.

"Yay!" I yelled because even though a bug on its back kicking its legs was still gross, it wasn't just a bug anymore, it was Spike.

"I knew you could do it!" TJ put his finger down into the hat and tipped Spike over so he could stand on his little spiky feet again. Then TJ tucked the hat up against his stomach to keep Spike safe, and we all hurried back to Professor Reese's.

TJ spent the rest of the afternoon giving us updates on Spike in his tank. "He's eating an apple slice," he told us as I cuddled Baxter. Meanwhile, Professor Reese was scribbling her notes as fast as she could because Spike was the first living being to teleport! And survive! Who knew a big bug would make scientific history!

"He's walking on the roof of his bark house," TJ said.

"Spike's all better." I smiled at Baxter.

He grinned back.

TJ probably would have stayed in the lab forever, telling us what Spike was doing, but I noticed on the clock that we'd been there a long time, maybe longer than Mom would think an opportunity to be dependable should take. "We better go home, TJ."

But when I noodled Baxter's ears to say good-bye, he whined and pulled his head away. "Oh! Professor Reese! I forgot to tell you—I think Baxter's ear is sick," and I told her how it had been bothering him all afternoon.

Professor Reese frowned. "Hmm. I'll keep an eye on him tonight."

I gave Baxter a little scritch between his shoulder blades. "I'll check on you tomorrow morning, OK?" I nodded, and Baxter nodded back.

That night after dinner, TJ worked on his stop-motion short. After 114 pictures, Caveman had run step by step across the table. Zombie Cheerleader had jumped out from behind the building. Now Caveman raised his club while Zombie Cheerleader whapped his head with her pom-poms.

Picture by picture, the battle was about to start.

I went into my room and walked over to the bookcase. I wanted to see what the dog books said about ear infections. Baxter had two of the symptoms: shaking his head and scratching his ear. Plus, he didn't like getting his ears noodled anymore. So even though none of the books mentioned noodle avoiding, I decided it was a symptom, too.

The next morning, me and TJ ran over to Professor Reese's.

She opened the door holding her crossword and wearing a red leotard and red footless tights, looking like an elf or maybe a fire hydrant. "Hi, Jordie. Hi, TJ."

"How's Spike?" TJ asked before I had a chance to even ask about Baxter.

"Spike seems fine," Professor Reese said. "Right now, he's enjoying a slice of banana from my morning cereal."

So TJ ran down to the lab to see, and I hugged Baxter gently around the middle. Professor Reese turned to me. "You were right, Jordie. Baxter's ear was bothering him all night."

"Aw, you poor thing!" I petted him but not near his ears.

"I just made an appointment for the vet to see him at three fifteen," she went on. "Can you walk Baxter to the vet's after school, and I'll meet you there?"

"Of course!" I kissed him right between his crazy eyebrows—a kiss to help him feel better. Then I yelled down the basement stairs for TJ, and we headed to school.

The whole way to school, I worried about Baxter. And my mood didn't get any better when I realized it was already Wednesday, which meant our second week of Study Buddies was almost over. Tyler hadn't gotten in trouble on Monday or Tuesday, but that was only because Mrs. Wilson had kept an eagle eye on Tyler's group the whole time: every time Tyler or one of his kids looked up from the assignment, they'd shrink back like a mouse who didn't want to get gulped.

And now we only had a few days left because at the Good-bye–Hello Ceremony next Monday, me and Tyler would say good-bye to the second graders, and then they'd say hello to the new Buddies.

Just a few days left, and Tyler was *wasting* his.

"This is so *stupid*, this is just *baby* stuff," he moaned as we walked up our hallway. "*Stupid* baby drawings," he said about the penguins (on icebergs) the second graders had drawn that were posted in their hallway. But I thought the drawings were adorable and that Tyler was the one who was stupid.

We were supposed to help our groups practice presenting A Special Person in My Life in an "appropriate manner," which I decided meant "nice and loud."

Katie did fine. She was already pretty loud, so she only

needed to practice once. Helping Maya was tougher because she was so shy. She had ideas she wanted to share about her Special Person, but she stared at the floor the whole time. All you could see was the top of her head, and you couldn't hear her at all.

But just before it was time to present, I figured out a way to make it better maybe. "I'll sit in the middle of the back row. Just look at me when you say it, OK?"

The whole class gathered on the rug in front of the classroom, with me and Tyler smooshed in with the back row of kids. It was so smooshed that I had kids practically stepping on my hands and sitting on my feet to fit us all on the rug.

First Katie did hers on her grandma, and she was nice and loud and appropriate. Then Maya got up. At first, she looked so hard at the floor that you could see the top of her head almost all the way to the back of her neck.

But then I guess she suddenly remembered what I had told her because she looked up. When Maya saw all the people, her eyes got huge, but then she found me in the back row. I nodded and gave her a big smile. She looked straight at me and talked about her baby sister so appropriately, we could even hear what she was saying. I clapped louder than anyone when she was done.

Chloe and Logan did OK in their presentations, but

Tyler himself wasn't doing that great, sitting in the audience. All of us smooshed together so much was just too much for Tyler: he kept poking a kid in front of him to make him giggle.

"Tyler . . ." Mrs. Wilson said. She eagle-eyed him from across the room.

"I didn't do anything!"

When the presentations were done, Mrs. Wilson walked over to Tyler. I heard her say to him in a low voice, "I expect more from you, Tyler. I expect better. But I also believe in you. I believe you can be an outstanding Study Buddy, and I'm looking forward to seeing that tomorrow."

And Tyler didn't say anything to me the whole way back to class.

For the rest of the day, Tyler seemed quieter than usual. But as soon as the final bell rang, I didn't have time to think about it anymore. I needed to get home to take Baxter to the vet.

When me and TJ opened Professor Reese's back door, Baxter came out to meet us. But he wasn't bounding-out-of-the-house happy, he was only achy-ear-but-still-a-little-bit happy.

I looked in Baxter's eyes. "You're not feeling better, are you?" I shook my head.

Baxter shook his head.

"It doesn't look like you want to be King of the Bounce today." I shook my head again.

He shook his head even harder than I did because he had achy ears attached to his—and head shaking was another symptom the books talked about.

TJ gave him a little pat and then went downstairs to say hi to Spike. I stayed upstairs, cuddling Baxter to cheer him up, but he just scratched his ear and whined.

At three o'clock, I yelled down to TJ, "Time to go!"

"I want to stay here with Spike!"

"This counts as our walk, TJ." And then I added, "Baxter's ear is really gross!" because TJ likes gross, goopy stuff.

"OK." He came up the stairs.

As we hurried over to the vet's, I worried even harder because it seemed like Baxter was tilting his head, which was *another* symptom the books talked about.

When we got to the vet's, we sat on the waiting room bench, with Baxter on one side of me with his head in my lap and TJ on the other side, jiggling his legs. While we waited, I read Baxter the pamphlets on the waiting room table to distract him and chose the grossest, goopiest ones so that TJ would like them, too.

When Professor Reese got there, the receptionist handed her a clipboard with a patient information sheet. Professor Reese filled out her address and phone number. The receptionist weighed Baxter, and we found out he weighed 78 pounds (which is actually more than TJ). She wrote that on the chart, too.

Then she brought us into the examination room.

The vet, Dr. Sheffield, came in and said hello. He looked over the chart and noticed the space for a microchip ID number was blank. "Let's write it down and get you registered," Dr. Sheffield said. "If Baxter ever gets lost, it will be easier to identify him." He opened a drawer and pulled out a thing that looked sort of like a TV remote.

I'd read about microchips in my dog books, but I'd never seen the scanner way up close. "How does it work?"

So Dr. Sheffield explained: a microchip, which is the size of a grain of rice, is inserted under the skin between the shoulder blades with a big needle—

"Cool!" TJ said.

—and it contains a unique identification number: a different number for every dog. When you run the scanner over the shoulder blades, it activates the chip, which transmits a radio wave showing the ID number (so now I knew another thing the waves on Professor Reese's posters did). The scanner displays the number on its LCD screen, and that's how a vet knows it's your Baxter and not somebody else's.

When Dr. Sheffield waved the microchip scanner over

Baxter's shoulder blades, he paused. He studied the number on the screen and said, "Hmm." He frowned. "Baxter's chip isn't working right."

"How do you know?" I asked.

"See the number?"

Me and TJ crowded in. TJ read out the number on the LCD screen. "45530313."

"A standard microchip has between nine and fifteen digits, but this number only has eight. So it's not a standard microchip." Dr. Sheffield shook his head. "There was a company a few years ago that went into business with a new design—a programmable microchip. The idea was that people could program the chip with their phone number. But the company used cheap parts. A lot of the microchips didn't work reliably—like this one—and the company went out of business."

"But how do you know Baxter's chip isn't working right?" I asked.

"Well, look at the number. It's not a phone number because those are seven digits long or ten with the area code. And it doesn't look like a street address." He looked back up at us. "Frankly, I don't know what this number is."

"Yeah, I don't know either," TJ said.

Dr. Sheffield shrugged. "I'll go ahead and write it in the chart, but you might consider having this chip removed and a standard chip inserted. It's a small surgical procedure that most dogs tolerate well."

"Another time, perhaps," Professor Reese said. "I don't want to do anything else to Baxter while he's not feeling well."

"Fair enough." Dr. Sheffield nodded. "All right, let's take a look at those ears."

He opened a drawer and pulled out an ear-looker thingy, which he called an otoscope, and when I said I wanted to be a vet, he let me look. It was even cooler than looking through Professor Reese's spectrometer (though Baxter's ear canal was so red and oozy that I didn't think it would be ending up on a poster any time soon).

"Do you want to be a vet, too?" Dr. Sheffield smiled at TJ.

He shook his head. "No way. I'm going to make movies."

"But he likes gross stuff," I added, and I stepped back so TJ could take a look.

TJ peered in Baxter's ear. "Ewww! Awesome!"

"There's definitely an infection in the right ear," Dr. Sheffield said. "And the left ear is looking a little inflamed, so I think we better treat both." He cleaned Baxter's ears and showed us how to use some ear ointment and gave us a copy of his report with instructions written on it for how to take care of his ears. "Between the infection and the

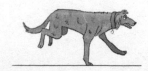

ointment, Baxter's hearing may be affected for a few days, but he'll be feeling better in no time."

We were extra careful walking home to go nice and slow and let Baxter sniff as much as he wanted. When people stopped us to ask if they could pet him, I said temporarily no, because I was afraid they would bang into his ears by mistake, but that if they saw us again in a few days, then yes, of course, absolutely.

But when we crossed the park, Tyler came over from the basketball court. He knelt down and put out his hand for Baxter to sniff.

"Be careful of his ears—" I started to say, but Tyler was already petting him.

Only he was petting Baxter so gently that after a minute, Baxter closed his eyes. "Who's a good boy?" Tyler said quietly.

Then he stood up. "You want to shoot some hoops?" he asked TJ.

"Yeah!"

"See ya later, Jordie," Tyler said as they started jogging over to the court.

"Tell Mom I'll be home in ten minutes!" TJ added.

"Who was that?" Professor Reese asked as we started walking again.

"Oh, that's just Tyler from my class," I said. "He's the

one I told you about—the worst kid in . . . in the whole class . . ." Only as I was saying it, it felt kind of funny because he'd just been so gentle with Baxter.

"That's the boy you were telling me about?" she asked.

"Yeah . . ." But it still felt funny. "I guess he *is* good with dogs."

Professor Reese nodded. "Indeed."

15

THE BARFING
SOCK-SNAKE

When we got home from the vet, I put the ear ointment and the copy of the vet report on the Baxter Station. I pulled more blankets out of the linen closet and made his beds extra smooshy, so they would be nice and soft—because even a magical dog needs extra smoosh when he's not feeling well.

I tucked Baxter into his bed in the lab and snuggled the blankets around him so he wouldn't get cold.

"I'll take good care of him tonight, Jordie." Professor Reese smiled.

So I gave Baxter the tiniest, carefulest kiss right between his crazy eyebrows, and his kiss back landed on my chin. "Get well soon."

Then I ran home. I wanted to tell Mom about Baxter and all the ways I'd been dependable—because usually she was the one who thought up great opportunities, but she'd been at work the whole time for this one. If I didn't tell her, how would she know?

So I described getting Baxter to the vet's on time and learning how to take care of his ear and then bringing him home and settling him into bed after.

"It sounds like you took great care of him, sweetie," she said.

By the time I got done telling her everything, TJ was already back and working on his short. I went into his room.

"How was shooting hoops with Tyler?"

TJ shrugged. "Fine."

Caveman and Zombie Cheerleader were in the middle of a battle. Caveman knocked one pom-pom away with his club, Zombie Cheerleader was bending over to pick it up, and TJ was taking picture after picture to capture it all.

"What's his movie about?" I asked.

"Whose?" TJ snapped another picture.

"Tyler's. In Video Club."

TJ looked up from his camera. "It's about this dirty sock that slides down off Tyler's foot and slithers around his room, eating little toys on the floor. The sock gets bigger

and bigger, and then it gets so big it barfs all the toys back out. Then it slides back onto Tyler's foot again." TJ laughed.

He turned back to the battle, lifting Caveman's foot a tiny bit, getting it ready to kick Zombie Cheerleader in the butt.

"Oh," I said.

Tyler's movie sounded really funny. All through dinner, I thought about the sock slithering around the floor, eating toys and then barfing them back up.

"Are you OK, honey?" Mom asked.

I nodded. "Yeah."

After dinner, I went into my room and grabbed my dog books. I figured I should read about microchips and otoscopes. But every time I tried to concentrate, I ended up staring out the window.

At bedtime, Mom came in and gave me a kiss. "Don't worry, Baxter will be well soon," and I realized that I hadn't even been thinking about Baxter.

I'd been thinking about Tyler.

He got in trouble at school, all the time.

But he'd been so good with Baxter, petting him so nicely.

Mrs. Wilson had been so mad at him during Study Buddies that she glared her eagle eye at him.

But he'd been nice to TJ, inviting him to shoot hoops.

And his movie sounded really good.

How could Tyler be the worst kid in the whole class sometimes and then at other times not seem that way at all?

It was so confusing that I was still thinking about it the next morning. I ate my breakfast superfast. "I'm going over to Dad's!" I yelled to Mom. And before she could say it, I added, "Seven fifteen on the nose!"

Then I ran over there.

I made my hot chocolate and then settled on the couch with Dad, who was drinking his coffee.

"Did you get in trouble a lot at school?" I asked him.

"Sometimes. It depended on the class." He smiled. "I liked band practice and choir." He set down his cup and picked up his guitar. "Why do you ask? Is something wrong?"

"No." I shrugged. "I'm just figuring things out."

Dad nodded. "Me too, kiddo. Me too." Then he began to play.

I leaned back and listened, wondering if Dad's getting in trouble was the same as Tyler's. And also wondering how you could be a grown-up and still be figuring things out.

Then Dad said, "What time is it?"

I checked the clock: 7:12. "Gotta go!"

I still hadn't figured out Tyler, but if *Dad* was still figuring things out and he was a *grown-up*, there was no way I

could figure out all of Tyler in just one morning. Besides, I had something way more important to do before school: I'd promised Baxter I'd check on him and see how he was feeling.

TJ was a slowpoke like always until I leaned over and whispered in his ear, "I wonder how Spike is feeling this morning." Then he sped up.

We were so early that when Professor Reese opened the door in her lavender leotard and footless tights (looking a little bit like an Easter egg), she invited us in.

TJ ran down to the lab to check on Spike, and I went straight to Baxter.

The vet was right that Baxter's hearing might be affected. Professor Reese had moved his bed from the bedroom down into the living room so he could doze while she did her yoga. He was dozing so hard that he didn't even notice me until I knelt down next to him.

"Your ears aren't all better yet, are they?" I shook my head.

Baxter shook his head—only once he started, he shook it extra long and hard because he was trying to shake the ache out of his ears.

"I need to put in the ointment," Professor Reese said. "Would you like to help?" So she did the left ear, and then I did the right one.

Professor Reese went back to doing her yoga and cross-word puzzle like normal (or as normal as things could be considering it was Professor Reese) while I petted and patted everywhere but Baxter's ears. And pretty soon he was dozing again.

"What's an eleven-letter word for 'prone to fussiness'?" she asked. "It needs to end in *y*."

"Superfussy?"

"That's only ten letters." She frowned. "Hmmm . . ." Then she bent into downward dog to think about it, and I snuggled Dozing Dog to help him feel better.

"Are we going to be teleporting the hat while Baxter is sick?" I asked.

"Persnickety!" She stood back up and wrote it in 7-across. "No. I want to give Baxter a few days off. But I came to a big realization last night. All this time, we've been looking at the situation from Baxter's point of view. Last night, I finally figured out a way to look at it from the hat's." She smiled, and her eyes got sparkly.

"Cool," I said, and I wondered now that I was her lab assistant if maybe my eyes were sparkly, too.

"I'm a little nervous about pulling it off," Professor Reese added—which surprised me, as she never seemed nervous about anything. "But mostly I'm very excited. I think we'll learn a lot." She smiled. "I'll tell you about it this afternoon."

16

BOUNCE-PASS KEEP-AWAY

When I got to school, I ran over to Megan and Aisha and Jasmine, by the bars. I told them about looking through the otoscope at Baxter's ear and putting in the ear ointment.

"Aw, poor Baxter!" Aisha said.

"Give him a big kiss for me!" Jasmine said. Then she and Aisha grabbed their backpacks and ran toward the classroom.

Me and Megan trailed behind. "I wish I could come over after school to help him feel better," she said.

"Me too."

Megan shrugged. "I asked my mom last night if I could come over to your house today before my lesson, but she said we have to go shopping for a new dress for my recital."

"Ooh. That's exciting."

She sighed. "Not really." The bell rang. "I don't really like piano that much—it's my mom who wants me to play." Then she ran toward class.

I couldn't believe it! Megan's lessons always sounded like so much fun—I didn't know she was stuck doing one she didn't even like!

I ran to the classroom and sat down in my seat. All during language arts, I thought about how some people— like Dad—would probably love piano lessons, but Megan didn't.

I wondered if you ever started something that you didn't like and you kept doing it, you might start to like it later. But I also wondered if you tried something for a while and still didn't like it, if it was OK to quit. And how long you had to keep not liking it before you could quit and try something else you might like better.

It was all very confusing.

As Mrs. A. dismissed the rest of the class for recess, I realized that must be how Tyler felt about Study Buddies. I loved it, but it had been almost two weeks now, and it still didn't seem like he liked it at all. But Tyler didn't have to decide when to quit because our two weeks were almost over.

"I bet you're glad that Study Buddies is almost done," I said to Tyler as we walked up one hallway and down the other toward the second-grade classrooms.

But he just shrugged and said, "I don't know." And when we got there, he just sat down quietly in a little chair.

Katie and Maya ran over to hug me, and Mrs. Wilson said, "OK, class, let's head outside," because the Study Buddies session, it turned out, was PE. "We're working on basic ball skills like throwing and catching. So just take your groups and play ball."

Tyler's eyes got big. "That's it? Just play ball?"

Mrs. Wilson nodded.

I got Katie and Maya and me all set up in a triangle so that we could practice throwing and catching the ball, but when I looked over, Tyler was doing this cool thing with his group: bounce-pass keep-away, which he had made up right there on the spot. The rules were that the big player (say, Tyler) went running toward a little player (Logan or Chloe), and right when he almost got there, the little player did a bounce-pass under Tyler's hands to the other little player.

Logan and Chloe *loved* it! They loved how they could keep the ball away from a great big fifth grader. They kept laughing and laughing, and Tyler was laughing, too. It looked like way more fun than the boring pass-the-ball-around-the-triangle thing that I had set up. Katie and Maya must have thought so, too, because they ran over to play with Tyler's group. Soon, all four second graders were keeping the ball away from Tyler and laughing and laughing.

Meanwhile, I was just sort of standing there. I looked over and saw Mrs. Wilson smiling at Tyler, and suddenly I realized that at that very second, *Tyler was being a better Study Buddy than me.*

Just as I was getting ready to say to the kids, "How about I get in the middle now?" Mrs. Wilson told everyone that recess was over. So our Study Buddy session was done, too.

I tried to think of something quick I could do that was as good as what Tyler did, but all I could think of was to take Katie over to the classroom sink. The dirt and dust from bouncing the ball on the playground were stuck to all her sticky parts, and her face was also dirty from where she scratched itches.

I asked her to wash her hands and then showed her how she could use the wet paper towel from drying her hands to wipe the dirt off her face, too.

"There, doesn't that feel better?" I asked, and she nodded yes, and when she hugged me good-bye it was less sticky, which was nice.

But that still wasn't as good as what Tyler had done.

Tyler high-fived Logan and Chloe, and as we were leaving, Mrs. Wilson said, "Nice work today, Tyler," like he really *had* been outstanding for once, instead of a pain in the you-know-what (his favorite word). "Thanks, Jordie," she added as she turned to the class.

And then I knew that Mrs. Wilson thought Tyler had done better, too, because "nice work" is better than "thanks." It was weird because everyone knew Tyler was the worst kid in the whole class, but he'd just done better than me.

Tyler smiled the whole way back to our classroom.

The rest of the morning, I sat in my seat, wondering how Tyler could have done better than me. At lunch with Megan and Jasmine and Aisha, I wondered about it even harder.

After we finished eating, we went out like always to sit on the benches on the side of the school. Usually, I was too busy blabbing with them to pay much attention to who else was out on the playground. But I didn't feel like blabbing now.

I half listened to Aisha talk about shopping with her cousins to buy matching shirts while my eyes wandered around the monkey bars and slides, out across the soccer field . . . until I saw Tyler, walking over to the basketball courts.

Instead of stopping at the tall hoop for the big kids, he

kept walking until he got to the shorter one for the little kids.

"What's he doing?" I stood up.

"Who?" Megan asked.

Little kids started running over to him, and when I looked even harder I realized it was Mrs. Wilson's class! I hadn't noticed they had afternoon recess at the same time as our lunch period, but Tyler had noticed.

"Who are you looking at?" Megan asked again, but I was already walking toward them.

"Jordie, where are you going?" Megan called after me.

"My Study Buddies are on the playground!"

I walked faster as Tyler started teaching the second graders how to shoot baskets, the whole class waiting to try—including Katie and Maya!

Just as I reached the courts, Mrs. Wilson called the kids over to head back to class. Their recess was done. I only had time to wave to Katie and Maya before they went inside.

Tyler had been a better Study Buddy than me twice in one day!

It bugged me so much the rest of the afternoon that by the time the bell rang, all I wanted to do was go home and cuddle Baxter.

I walked extra fast, ignoring TJ every time he said, "Wait up!"

When we got home, TJ made a beeline for the cereal, but I didn't want a snack. I said, "I'm going to get Baxter for our walk."

I hurried over to Professor Reese's. But when I took the key from under the begonia and opened the back door, Baxter didn't come bounding out.

I walked into the kitchen. "Baxter!" I called as I walked through the dining room into the living room.

He was curled up on his smooshy bed by the purple couch.

"Wake up, Baxter!" I said.

His head popped up. He sleepy scrambled to his feet and rushed over, his tail wagging a million times a minute.

"Wow, your ears must really be bothering you—you didn't hear me come in at all, did you?"

I shook my head, and Baxter shook his head, too, flapping his ears extra hard because they still hurt. I gently hugged him around the tummy, and he leaned into me and rested his chin on my shoulder to hug me back.

And soon, I was feeling the tiniest bit better—because I realized that all the outstanding stuff Tyler had just done was with a basketball. So even if he was a better Basketball Study Buddy, I was still better than him in all the nonbasketball parts.

I stood up. "Let's get TJ."

Baxter followed me into the kitchen. I grabbed the leash from the Baxter Station and we headed out, closing the back door behind us.

But just as we came around the side of the house into Professor Reese's front yard, there was a man in a brown suit storming up the walk.

Baxter gave a little woof, deep in his throat.

The man glared at Baxter and me. Then he marched up Professor Reese's porch steps and rapped on the door.

17

THE CRABBY DETECTIVE

Baxter woofed hello and ran to see who the man was.

He rapped on Professor Reese's front door again, and by then Baxter was charging up the porch steps so he could sniff who the man was, too.

The man took a few steps backward, so I whistled Baxter back to me. Because even though he's the sweetest dog ever, he's a lot of dog when he meets you all at once.

The man reached into his pocket and pulled out a badge. "I'm Detective John Jacobs of the Portland Police Department. I'm looking for Margery Reese."

I shook my head. "She's not home."

He stuck the badge back in his pocket. "And who are *you* exactly?"

"Jordie Marie Wallace. I live next door."

I pointed toward our house, but the detective didn't even look. Instead, he said, "Has anything out of the ordinary happened around here recently?"

I didn't know how to answer that because lately it seemed like *everything* was out of the ordinary. But of course I couldn't say *that*. But I didn't think I should lie to the police, either, so I tried to figure out something to say that was true but not too teleport-y.

I patted Baxter's shaggy neck. "Well, yes," I finally decided. "I got half of a magical dog—"

The detective raised his finger to cut me off. "Out of the ordinary for *Mrs. Reese*."

"*Professor* Reese," I corrected him, as politely as I could (which, if you're a kid correcting a grown-up, they never think is polite enough). "She likes to be called *Professor*. She says no one ever thinks that a little old lady could be a scientist and that it's good to challenge assumptions."

"Fine." He took a deep breath. "Has anything out of the ordinary happened recently to *Professor* Reese?"

"Yes. She got half of a magical dog, too. The other half." I scritched Baxter's back while he sniffed and sniffed in the detective's direction. "Technically, he sleeps at her house, but *I* take care of him in the afternoon—which is half the day, if you think about it, so he's half hers and half mine."

I stopped talking, as it didn't seem like the detective was listening anymore.

"Are your parents home?"

"No."

He went back down the porch steps and started wandering around Professor Reese's yard.

"My mom'll be home soon," I added as me and Baxter wandered after him.

The detective looked in all the windows. Then he squatted down, and Baxter helped him peer into the dark crawlspace beneath her porch.

"What are you looking for?" I asked.

But he just stood back up and put his hands on his hips, glancing over his left shoulder and then his right. "*Un*believable," he muttered to himself. "Not even missing twenty-four hours yet."

"Professor Reese is missing?" My stomach started feeling fluttery.

He shook his head. "Probably just went shopping and forgot to tell anyone." He squinted up at the second story. "But does that matter? Of course not. *One call* from the president of the university to the police chief, and I'm pulled off all my other cases."

"Wait. You mean she's *missing person* missing or more like she's not at work and nobody knows where she—"

"And *whose* butt's in a sling if anything happens to her?" He marched back up the front porch steps. "*My* butt, who else."

Which of course made me look at his butt.

He rang the doorbell, twice.

Baxter gave a little woof.

"She's not home," I said again, and now it felt scary saying it, even though it hadn't felt scary before.

He turned to me, whipped a little notepad and pencil out of his jacket pocket, and flipped to a fresh page. "OK, when's the last time you saw her?"

"This morning, before I went to school."

He wrote that down.

I hurried up the steps to see what he was writing. Baxter came with me. "Did something happen to her?" And my stomach felt jumpy even *asking*.

"I don't know yet. *That's why I'm investigating.*" He held up his notepad to prove it. "What was she doing the last time you saw her?"

"Yoga and a crossword puzzle."

He frowned. "At the same time?"

"Well, mostly the crossword but she does downward-facing dog pose when she can't figure out a word. She says the blood flow is good for the brain."

"Of course she does." He rubbed his forehead like it hurt.

"And what was she wearing?"

"A lavender leotard. And those tights with no feet at the bottom."

"Are you sure your parents aren't home?" he asked again.

I nodded.

"Fine. Footless tights." He added it to his list. "So what were you doing in her yard just now?"

"Hanging out with Baxter."

The detective's head shot up, and his eyes narrowed. "Baxter? Who's that?" He wrote *BAXTER* in capital letters on his pad and underlined it, twice.

I pointed.

"The dog?"

"Yes. Baxter." I gave him a soft little scritch on top of the head (Baxter's, not the detective's). He likes that.

The detective stabbed at the doorbell a few times.

"The *back* door is unlocked," I said.

"*Un*believable." He stomped around to the back.

Baxter and I hurried after him.

He knocked on the back door and yelled, "Portland Police Department!"

"She's not h—" I started to say again, but by then he was asking if I had permission to enter the premises (which I did) and if I had noticed any signs of a disturbance (which I hadn't). "I didn't go through the whole house, though.

Just the middle part."

"Hmm." He opened the back door and stuck his head in. "Margery Reese! This is Detective John Jacobs of the Portland Police Department! I'm coming in to do a wellness check!" Then he pushed the door all the way open. "I'm coming in now!"

But me and Baxter didn't follow him because now the idea of going into the house felt kind of scary. We stood at the doorway, looking into the kitchen at the black-and-white floor checkered like a big chessboard and the white cupboards, thick with paint. "Everything looks normal," I said. "That's good, right?"

But instead of answering, he just walked through the dining room and on into the living room.

"I'm coming upstairs now!" I heard him yell.

A few minutes later, he came back into the kitchen. "No one's home."

"Did you check the basement?" I asked. "Her lab is down there. . . ."

So he stomped off again.

I hugged Baxter close to me until the detective came back, shaking his head. "The house is empty."

"She was fine this morning," I said as he pushed past me, back outside.

He stopped in the driveway and flipped to the first page

of his notepad. I hurried over to see what he'd already written:

MARGERY REESE—MISSING ALL DAY—MISSED TWO CLASSES
AND DEPARTMENT MEETING
ATYPICAL BEHAVIOR—USUALLY VERY RESPONSIBLE
NO ANSWER ON HER HOME PHONE

"And does she have a *cell* phone?" he muttered. "*Of course not*. That would be *too easy*."

"She thinks cell phone radiation is bad for the brain," I started to explain, but then I stopped. I didn't think he wanted to hear any more of the professor's theories on brains. He looked like his brain was about to explode.

He now added to the list:

NO SIGN OF FORCED ENTRY OR FOUL PLAY IN HOUSE

He frowned at me again. "So *nothing* out of the ordinary happened in the past twenty-four hours?"

"Ordinary for Professor Reese or ordinary for everyone else?"

He glared at me and shoved his notepad back in his pocket. Then he handed me a business card with his phone number. "If you think of anything really important, call me." He stormed off. "And have your parents call me!"

Baxter and I followed him all the way to his car, my stomach curling into a tight little knot. "Hey, you're going to find her, right? 'Cause my half of Baxter is fine, but Professor Reese's half is starting to get worried."

"I'll do my best!" He yanked open his car door, climbed in, and slammed it closed.

I scratched Baxter's fuzzy neck as the detective drove away. "Don't worry. It'll be OK."

Baxter looked up at me, raising one eyebrow and then the other. He didn't quite believe me, and I didn't quite believe me, either.

I slid the detective's card into my pocket.

A lot *out of the ordinary* had happened since Professor Reese moved in, but I didn't know if I'd bother to call the detective. Because if he didn't think that a magical dog was *really important*, I was pretty sure I'd have to find Professor Reese myself.

18

BAXTER SLUMBER PARTY

After the detective left, I sat down in the grass, rubbed Baxter's tummy, and tried to think the whole thing through. There was plenty of stuff that seemed *really important*—important enough to tell a police detective looking for a missing professor.

The problem was, even if I *did* decide to break my promise to Professor Reese not to tell anyone about T-waves and her experiments, I knew the detective wouldn't believe a word of it, seeing as how he had no interest in a magical dog, even, and this was way more complicated.

And there was no way I could prove any of it, anyway: I didn't know how to work the teleportation machine because Professor Reese always set everything up. All I could show him was a map with a bunch of pins stuck in it, and I had a feeling that wouldn't be enough.

Besides, I didn't know just how *missing* Professor Reese was—if she was missing like a missing person, or just missing like maybe she'd gotten all caught up in work and was actually sitting in a little room somewhere, staring into a spectrometer and not finishing her sentences. Because it was still light out—it wasn't even dinnertime yet—and sometimes she worked way later. The detective seemed more *annoyed* than anything else, so I didn't know yet how worried I needed Baxter and me to be.

"Come on, Baxter," I said, standing up and, I realized, waking him up, because I'd been thinking for a while and rubbing his tummy the whole time.

I tucked him back into Professor Reese's house. "I'll be back soon, OK?" I nodded.

He nodded back.

Then I ran home.

TJ was at his desk, snapping a picture. "Come look! Zombie Cheerleader just knocked down Caveman. She's going to try and eat his brains!"

I hurried over. "You won't believe what just happened!" I told him everything that had happened.

TJ didn't seem as worried as I was that Professor Reese wasn't home. "She's probably working or something." He

151

was mad he missed the police detective, though. He asked me three times if I had gotten to ride in the police car with the siren going, and I said no the third time, too.

Then Mom came home, carrying a bag of groceries.

"There was a cop talking to Jordie!" TJ said.

"What?!"

I told Mom about the detective, as I handed over his card.

She went straight into the kitchen, set the groceries on the counter, and picked up the phone. "Detective John Jacobs, please . . . Yes, this is Susan Wallace. My daughter Jordie said you asked me to call? . . . Yes, Jordie said you spoke with her for quite some time . . ."

And then she started frowning until she burst out, "Yes, that's true, but she's also very bright!" She sounded annoyed, and TJ's eyes got big because Mom was yelling at a cop. "All right, fine!"

She hung up the phone and turned to me. "What did you say to that detective?"

"I didn't say anything!" I plopped down in a kitchen chair. "I tried to, but he wouldn't listen to me."

Mom nodded. "He didn't listen to me much, either." She sat down at the kitchen table. "The detective said he was trying to track down her family members and asked us to let him know if she comes home."

"But what if she doesn't?"

Mom put her hand on top of mine. "I'm sure she's just fine. Grown-ups have all sorts of things they need to do. I wouldn't worry, honey. I'm sure she'll be home soon."

"I guess." I stood up. "I didn't get a chance to take Baxter on his walk. I was too busy talking to the detective."

"OK," Mom said. "Dinner will be ready in about half an hour."

"Come on, TJ," I said.

We walked over to Professor Reese's and grabbed Baxter. "Let's walk around the neighborhood and see if anyone's seen her."

We stopped everyone we saw, and even went into all the stores, to see if anyone had seen Professor Reese earlier in the day.

"Who?" almost everyone one asked.

As soon as I said "the old lady I share this dog with," almost everybody knew exactly who I meant—because Baxter was pretty hard not to notice when he walked by, and once you noticed him, you never forgot him.

But no one had seen her all day.

We brought Baxter back to Professor Reese's house and headed home. Mom was just finishing making spaghetti (which I love, even though it's gross to watch TJ eat it).

I sat down at the kitchen table. TJ sat down, too, and

started playing with his paper napkin, tearing it into long thin strips. Usually, that drives Mom crazy because he leaves shreds of napkin all over the floor, but this time she didn't notice.

She gave me a quick hug. "Try not to worry, honey. I'm sure Professor Reese is fine."

Suddenly, I had a terrible thought. "What if she doesn't come home tonight?" I asked.

"I'm sure if she doesn't then there's a good reason," Mom said.

"I meant, what about Baxter? He'll be alone all night," I said. "And his ears are sore. He needs company."

"I'm not sleeping in that big empty house," TJ blurted out, and little pieces of napkin flew everywhere.

"I'm sorry, Jordie, but you know Baxter can't sleep in our house." Mom forked pasta onto our plates, ladled on the sauce, and added salad on the side. "He's a dog. He'll be fine."

"But he's a *sick* dog," I said. "He'll be lonely."

I twirled my spaghetti around and around on my fork and thought.

Then I got an idea—a *great* idea. I jumped up and ran to the phone and called Dad and told him to come right over, because we needed his help—

"Jordie, what's going on?" Mom asked.

"Hang on," I said. I got another plate and filled it with spaghetti and sauce and salad, and by then Dad was coming into the kitchen saying, "What's up?"

That's when I unveiled my great idea: a Baxter Slumber Party, which I wanted to wait to mention until Dad got there—it was the kind of thing he might say yes to at the same time Mom said no, and then I had a fifty-fifty chance. "'Cause the landlord said no dogs in the *house*," I explained. "He didn't say no dogs in the *garage*."

"We're having a slumber party in the garage?" TJ said. "Cool!"

"Actually, he was pretty clear about his 'no dog policy,'" Mom said.

"But it's not like Baxter is *living* here—he's just *visiting*, like a guest," I said. "It'll just be for one night. *Please?* Me and TJ and Baxter can sleep on camping pads on the floor, and Dad can have the spare cot, and Mom, you can stay in your nice soft bed in the house, if you'd be more comfortable there. And we'll see you in the morning, just like always."

I saved the best part for last: "It would be a great opportunity for me to be dependable because Professor Reese is depending on me to help take care of Baxter!"

Dad looked at Mom and shrugged. "What do you think? For one night only?"

"Great!" I said, because it sounded enough like a yes to me. I stood up and yanked TJ to his feet, too. "We'll get it all set up! You guys don't have to do anything!"

Then I pulled TJ out of the kitchen before Mom could say anything else.

It took until practically bedtime to set everything up perfectly—the pads and the sleeping bags, plus my dog books to read and the flashlights and the snacks. I ran over to Professor Reese's house, where Baxter met me at the door.

"You want to come to a slumber party, don't you?" I nodded.

Baxter nodded, too.

I left a note on the kitchen counter, just in case Professor Reese came home in the middle of the night, saying where Baxter was. I also got a can of dog food because I remembered no one had fed him dinner yet. I grabbed Baxter snacks and the ear ointment off the Baxter Station, piled everything on top of Baxter's bed, and dragged the whole thing back over to our garage. Baxter trotted in behind me, ate his dinner, and then plopped down on his bed like he'd been going to slumber parties his whole life.

I flipped through my dog books and read TJ all the parts on dog parasites, which were gross so I knew he'd like them. Then me and TJ ate all the snacks (except Baxter's) and went into the house to brush our teeth.

Mom and Dad came back out with us.

"How's King of the Bounce?" Dad asked. He patted Baxter's side and scratched between his shoulders.

"Not very bouncy," I said. "But he's happy about the slumber party."

Me, Baxter, TJ, and Mom climbed onto the big smooshy pile of sleeping bags and Baxter's bed. Dad turned on a flashlight, turned off the overhead light, and walked across the dark garage to join us. I told ghost stories (which TJ loves—the grosser and goopier the better) holding the flashlight under my chin to make my face glow green, which makes them extra scary.

Finally, it got so late that TJ lay down to listen. After a while, his eyes started to close.

"Time for bed." Mom kissed the top of my head and the top of TJ's head and went into the house. I lay down in my sleeping bag, snuggling up next to Baxter.

Dad settled down in a camp chair. He turned the flashlight off and played his guitar very, very quietly, because he always stays up late, and it was only about nine. But he doesn't mind sitting in the dark and playing his guitar, and sometimes he even does that on purpose.

I hugged Baxter extra close so that Professor Reese's half wouldn't be worried either, snuggling up to his fuzzy back and waiting to get sleepy.

But TJ kept rustling around in his sleeping bag. "Cut it out! Quit panting on me!" (He was on the dog-breath side of Baxter, not the fuzzy side.)

So Dad turned the garage light on, and TJ moved his sleeping bag over to the other side of me, so then I was in the middle. Dad turned the light back off and went back to playing his guitar.

Dad played so quietly that sometimes I could barely hear the music at all as I drifted in and out—first I'd notice it, then I wouldn't, then I would again. And resting my head against Baxter's scruffy back, it seemed like he was humming in his sleep, ever so faintly. I put my ear down by his shoulder blades, and sure enough, there was a faint hum coming from his microchip, which was weird.

I thought, Maybe since the microchip is the kind with cheap parts that doesn't work right, it hums even though it's not supposed to.

But it didn't matter anyway because it wasn't an annoying hum—it was more like he was just humming along with the music. It was so nice and peaceful that as I fell asleep, I was *almost* positive everything would be fine in the morning and that Professor Reese would be home.

19

JORDIE, *JORDIE . . .* JORDIE!

But when Baxter and I went over to Professor Reese's the next morning to get his breakfast, the newspaper was sitting on the porch, which meant: no crossword puzzle, no yoga, no footless tights—

No Professor Reese.

Only we'd all slept so badly on our camping pads—with TJ saying, "Scoot over!" a million times—that we kept waking up. When we *did* finally stay asleep, we overslept.

So me and TJ didn't have time to do anything about the no Professor Reese. TJ only had time to run down to the lab and give Spike an orange slice while I fed Baxter his breakfast and did his ear ointment. Then we hurried to

school. All I could do was hope that she would come home during the day and have some ordinary-only-for–Professor Reese reason why she'd been gone all night.

My lousy day got worse because I remembered that it was Friday, and Megan was home with her grandparents. Plus, the bell was already ringing when I got there, so I had to run straight to class. I barely had time to tell Jasmine and Aisha about even half of the Baxter Slumber Party before Mrs. A. started blabbing—

"Jordie."

—like how we'd all piled onto the big pile of sleeping bags—

"Jordie . . ."

—and Baxter had climbed into the middle so we could all give him pets and pats—

"JORDIE."

—with Mrs. A. so impatient that I couldn't even finish.

And the lousiest thing of all was that it was my last Study Buddy session before the Good-bye–Hello Ceremony next week.

Tyler and I walked up one hallway and down the other. "You did good yesterday—your bounce-pass keep-away game was really fun," I said. "You did even better than me," I added, because it was true.

"What?"

"Pretty soon *you* could show someone how to be a good Study Buddy."

"Wait." He stopped walking and looked at me. "You think *you've* been helping *me?*"

"Well, maybe just a little—"

"Don't you *get* it, Jordie? Why do you think Mrs. A. picked us to do this?"

I didn't know if I should say it out loud: that since he was the worst kid in the whole class, she needed me to balance him out. But then I remembered her "Jordie-*Jordie*-JORDIE."

Tyler shook his head. "She thinks we're both losers." He started walking again.

I felt my face get hot, and it just got hotter and hotter as I hurried after him to Mrs. Wilson's classroom.

When we opened the door, Katie and Maya ran up and hugged *Tyler*, probably just because of bounce-pass keep-away—but still, they hugged him first.

Tyler froze and turned bright red, and Mrs. Wilson grinned.

I was sure that Katie and Maya were going to hug me next, only right then Mrs. Wilson motioned us over to an empty table. I thought, They just didn't have time to hug me because of Mrs. Wilson.

"Today we're working on one of our Keys for the

Classroom: helping others. Each group needs to create a poem or drawing about being helpful."

Katie and Maya said they wanted to do a drawing of someone who helped them. Mrs. Wilson got a big piece of construction paper. "Who do you want to draw?"

Katie cupped her not-as-sticky-as-they-used-to-be hands around Maya's ear, and whispered something, and Maya nodded. "It's a surprise," Katie said. They bent down low over the paper.

Tyler and Chloe and Logan were huddled together, whispering. Then he looked up. "We're doing a poem."

"Terrific!" Mrs. Wilson said, handing them a big piece of paper, too. "Please write it up to share with the class."

I sat down on one of the little chairs and watched Katie and Maya work. They drew a face with a big smile and started adding brown hair.

I thought, My hair is brown. I ran my fingers through it because I wanted it to look good in case it was me they were drawing.

They started working on the neck and arms.

Mrs. Wilson came over to check on us. "How's it going?"

"Good." I shrugged. "But they don't really need any help today," which made me feel a little weird because I was just sitting there like a bump.

"Awesome!" She smiled.

But it didn't *feel* awesome. I was just sitting there, not helping them at all.

As she walked over to see how things were going with Tyler, Katie and Maya added a blue shirt and blue pants to their drawing.

I thought, I'm wearing a blue shirt, and I'm wearing jeans! They *did* choose me!

I felt so good that I wanted to hug them. But they were hunched over busy, so instead I just said, "That looks great! Do you need help writing the name of the person at the bottom of the poster?"

Katie shook her head. "We already know how to write it." Which of course they would, since *Jordie* had been on the Study Buddy bulletin board for two weeks.

Then Katie wrote *Mrs.*

And that's when I noticed that Mrs. Wilson was wearing a blue shirt and blue pants, and her hair was brown, too.

Maya wrote *Wilson*, and she started so big that she had to curve the word around and run it down the side of the page, but it still fit. And then it was time to present to the class.

Mrs. Wilson asked Tyler's group to go first. Katie and Maya smooshed in with me on the rug, and I tried to feel good that they had done such a great job—drawing Mrs. Wilson.

Tyler and his group went up to the front. Logan and

Chloe held up their big sheet of paper and started to read their poem out to the class:

"He's really nice." (And when they read that, Tyler smiled.)

"Every day." (And his smile got bigger, like he was waiting. . . .)

"We Like him a lot." (And Logan's and Chloe's eyes got big. . . .)

He Plays ball with us." (And they started to giggle. . . .)

"HE's our Buddy." ("Not their Butt-y," Tyler said—and stuck his butt out!)

"TyleR!!!"

"Tyler!" Mrs. Wilson said while the whole class laughed.

And I expected him to say, "I didn't do anything!" but instead, he just grinned at her. And she was still trying not to crack up as she called Katie and Maya to the front of the room.

I didn't want to go up with them. I wanted to sit in the back and watch because I knew *I* wouldn't be making anybody laugh. I hadn't done anything at all the whole time—I'd just sat there, so what did they need me for? But Maya grabbed my hand, so I was stuck.

I stood up in front with Katie and Maya, feeling dumb, which *was* dumb because the only person who knew I had been thinking it would be me on the poster was *me*. So there wasn't any reason to be embarrassed, but, for some reason, I was anyway.

"This is Mrs. Wilson." Katie held up the picture. "She helps us every day with our reading and math, and sometimes she lets us feed the fish."

I tried to remind myself that *of course* they would have chosen Mrs. Wilson because she had been their teacher since school started. I'd only been their Study Buddy two weeks, and I didn't get to choose who fed the fish.

I made my mouth into a big smile while Katie said, "Mrs. Wilson is really fun. And she's really nice. And she reads us funny books." But my smile kept wavering like it didn't want to stay on my face anymore.

What I really wanted was to just go smoosh myself back on the rug again and let everyone step on me. But I was still a Study Buddy for two more minutes, so I tried to think about how I could help Katie and Maya. I realized that Maya hadn't said a word—how could she when she didn't have me in the audience to look at and not get scared while she talked?

So I leaned down and whispered in her ear, "Do you want to say something nice about Mrs. Wilson?"

She nodded. She took a deep breath. I felt her squeeze onto my hand harder, so I squeezed back. Maya said in a nice loud voice, "Mrs. Wilson helps us a lot."

Then she and Katie ran over and handed the drawing to her.

Mrs. Wilson said, "Thank you both so much!"

She pinned the poem and drawing on her special bulletin board behind her desk. And then it was time to leave.

Tyler made big burping noises the whole way back, but it didn't even bug me because I was too busy thinking about how that was *it*. Study Buddies was *over*, and all I'd done was make Maya a little less shy and Katie a little less sticky.

I felt sort of empty inside, and at lunch I wasn't even hungry, which was weird because you'd think if you were empty inside, you'd be starving.

When Mrs. A. dismissed the class for afternoon recess, she called me and Tyler up to her desk. "I just wanted to see how the Study Buddy program went."

"It was good," Tyler said.

I nodded. I wanted to say how much I'd loved helping Katie and Maya, but I couldn't get the words out.

"Mrs. Wilson told me you did an outstanding job being leaders in her class." Mrs. A. patted us both on the shoulder. "And I'm confident the experience will help you lead by example in *our* class, too—staying focused and getting your work done without disturbing others. Great job! I'm really proud of you!"

By the time she dismissed us for recess, my face felt so hot I thought it would melt my shirt.

Tyler ran to the basketball courts to join a game. I knew Aisha and Jasmine would be by the bars, but I walked in the other direction, all the way out to the soccer field, walking farther and farther.

Tyler was *right*: I hadn't been chosen first for Study Buddies because of my excellent people skills. Mrs. A. had chosen me and Tyler because she thought we were both losers!

I didn't even hear the whistle blow that recess was over. I only realized it when I looked up and there were only four kids still out on the playground—one of which of course was Tyler, which just proved it even more!

I had to run all the way back to class. Then I slumped down in my seat with Jasmine and Aisha staring at me with my face still all hot.

Aisha whispered, "Where were you at recess? Did Mrs. A. make you stay inside?"

But I just stared straight ahead at Mrs. A. like I hadn't heard her.

I didn't look at anyone, wondering if the whole class knew—Jasmine and Aisha and maybe even *Megan*. Maybe they'd known I was a loser all along. They were probably only being nice to me because their parents said they had to be nice to everyone, even losers. They probably forgot all about the vet/beauty parlor/day care the minute they got home.

I hated Study Buddies, and there was no way I was going to that stupid Good-bye–Hello Ceremony on Monday. I'd

go hide in the stupid bathroom.

As soon as the bell rang, I grabbed my backpack and hurried out of class.

TJ yakked about his short the whole way home, but I didn't say a word. I just ditched my backpack inside our front door and ran over to Professor Reese's.

I opened the door and ran into the living room. Baxter popped up in his bed.

"I need to ask you something, OK?" I nodded.

He nodded back.

I didn't know if Professor Reese was right—that it was just Baxter's mirror neurons making him nod—or if TJ was right—that Baxter was just doing what I did. Or if Baxter really, truly did understand me. I just knew I had to ask: "You still love me even though I'm a loser." And I couldn't help myself—I nodded long and hard. "Don't you?"

I took a deep breath.

And Baxter, he nodded back.

I threw my arms around him and buried my face in his fuzzy neck. I hugged him so long that after a while everything else fell away (except the faint hum from the microchip). It was just me, nose deep in warm dog, which smells nice (even though wet dog smells bad, which is weird because why would plain old water make you smell worse? Only somehow it does if you're a dog).

And pretty soon, I was feeling a tiny bit better.

I sat back on my heels and looked around. The late afternoon sun was coming in the living room windows, warming the old wood floors.

The first time I'd ever come into Professor Reese's house by myself, this room had felt museum empty, like nobody lived there. Now it felt empty again—because someone was missing.

"Did Professor Reese come home during the day?" I asked Baxter. "Let's see if she left a note."

Baxter followed me into the kitchen, but the counter was empty except for my note about the slumber party. "If she left a note, it's probably in the lab," I told him.

We walked down the stairs, but there was nothing, just the computers and the cables running everywhere and the teleporter and the electronic console with the lights and buttons, the big red one glowing like someone had pushed it on—

But never pushed it off.

And that's when I knew what had happened. Professor Reese had wanted to look at things from a different angle. She'd wanted to look at teleportation from the hat's point of view—and there was only one way to do that.

She'd teleported *herself.*

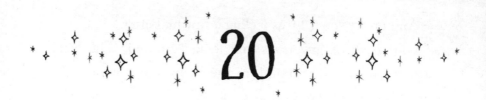

20

THE MISSING PROFESSOR

I sat down in the spinny chair, my own head spinning a little bit. Professor Reese had actually done it: she'd climbed into the teleporter and vibrated herself into a million little pieces. The million pieces had been picked up by the T-waves and plopped down somewhere else. And hopefully, the instructions had arrived via radio waves so she could put herself back together.

"But if she teleported herself," I said to Baxter as I scritched his ribs and thought it all through, "why didn't she just walk home afterward?"

Unless. Unless . . . something had gone wrong.

There were so many possibilities of what *could* go wrong. We'd teleported a hat. We'd teleported Spike (by accident). But even though Spike had survived, and even though he *seemed* fine, all we had to go on was how he acted.

Crawling on a stick and eating apple slices seemed way easier than all the things Professor Reese would need to be able to do when she'd landed—wherever she'd landed. Because who knew after being vibrated into a million little pieces and *POP*ped across town, if the reconfiguration instructions included reminding you that you were Professor Reese and you lived on Quimby Street and you should call Jordie and TJ and tell them you were OK.

That seemed like a lot for one little *beep–beep–boop* to accomplish.

I turned to Baxter. "We have to find her!"

We ran upstairs, and I clipped on his leash. Then we went over and got TJ, and I explained everything to him.

"Since she teleported herself, Baxter should be able to find her just like he always finds the hat," I said as we started to walk.

And walk.

And walk.

"C'mon, boy! Find Professor Reese!" I said. But Baxter wasn't galloping on the end of his leash. He just trotted along with us, stopping to sniff or, sometimes, shake his head because his ears were still itchy and hurt.

"Where are we going?" TJ finally asked. We'd been walking a long time.

"I don't know," I said. "I thought Baxter would have found her by now. But it doesn't even seem like he is looking." I wasn't sure Baxter was even magical anymore, except maybe it was because he wasn't feeling well.

I leaned over to hug him, and when I did, I noticed the microchip humming louder than when we left the house. And by the second hug a few blocks later, it was even *louder*, which was weird and made me think I'd need to tell Professor Reese if we found her—*when* we found her— that maybe she should get it removed after all because it sounded completely broken.

We walked and walked until our feet were sore.

"Maybe she teleported herself to Disneyland for vacation," TJ said. "That's what I'd do."

I shook my head. "I don't think she'd be thinking about vacation for her first teleportation. She'd want to get back home and write up her notes."

We kept walking until I didn't see any point to walking anymore. "Let's go back to the lab—maybe we missed something."

So we trudged back to Professor Reese's house. TJ grabbed a carrot for Spike and we went down into the lab.

We poked in drawers but just found office supplies. We

looked through files, but none of the papers said, "For my first experiment in human teleportation, I will send myself to . . ." though I was a teeny bit hoping.

"The computers are still on," TJ said. "Maybe we can look at the coordinates she used and find it on the map."

"Great idea!"

But when he tried, we found the screen password protected, so we couldn't see what she'd typed in. TJ tried to guess her password. He tried *654321*, then *123456*, and then even *Baxter*. But none of them worked.

Finally, TJ slumped down in the spinny chair and spun it slowly. I slumped down on the floor and leaned against a desk. Baxter slumped down next to me and put his head in my lap. And we all just slumped for a while, which didn't help anything.

Then the doorbell rang. Me and Baxter and TJ ran upstairs, and I think we were all half expecting to see Professor Reese standing there, even though I knew that was dumb because why would you ring the doorbell of your own house?

But instead it was Detective John Jacobs of the Portland Police Department. He scowled. "You again. *Figures*." He squinted at me. "What did you say your name was?"

"Jordie Marie Wallace," I said. "This is my brother, TJ. Did you find Professor Reese yet?"

"No." He scowled harder. "And *guess whose butt's* in a sling now?"

"Um, yours?" I said politely, because when a grown-up asks you a question you are supposed to answer it.

He glared at me (even though I'd been totally polite and he *had* asked). Then he put his hands on his hips and asked the same two questions over and over—had the professor come home, had she called—and I said no the fourteenth time, too.

He turned around and stomped down the porch steps, muttering, ". . . finally track down the daughter, and does *she* know anything? *Of course not—*"

"Wait!" I hurried after him. "Professor Reese has a daughter?" And I wondered if maybe she was in fifth grade like me.

He wheeled around. "Yes. A daughter. An *expert* in *international banking* who lives in *Australia—*"

Which made me realize that she must be a grown-up.

"Who is flying in *on Sunday* and expects *results!*" He put his hands on his hips again and glared at me and TJ and even at Baxter. "Are you *sure* there's nothing you can tell me?"

The situation was feeling more serious than when he'd asked me the day before. It made me even less sure of what I was supposed to do about the whole secret we weren't supposed to tell, but I didn't know if that meant even to the police.

So I tried to figure it out:

I'd just noticed the glowing red button a couple of hours ago. But even if I *did* point it out to the detective, I'd have to convince him it meant she'd teleported herself.

And then, of course, he'd ask us to prove it.

But if we tried to show him teleportation was real, all we could show him was the hat disappearing. We couldn't show him the hat landing on the other end because me and TJ couldn't see the password-protected coordinates, so we wouldn't know where we'd sent it. Plus, Baxter was sick, and he wasn't being very magical, which meant the Baxter part of teleportation wasn't working right now.

Besides, all the glowing and vibrating and popping and screaming might just make the detective think the teleporter was a hat-destroying Weapon of Mass Destruction. He might lock up the lab completely, and I didn't think that would help us find her.

I looked at TJ. He just shrugged. He didn't know, either.

But Professor Reese was missing, and everything felt too complicated, so I thought maybe I'd try a little bit, one more time. I took a deep breath. "Well, remember I started telling you yesterday about Baxter being magical—"

"*Un*believable!" Detective Jacobs turned and charged toward his car.

"Hey," TJ called after him. "Do you think I could ride in the police car with the siren going?"

Detective Jacobs barked out a laugh as he opened his car door. He climbed in and slammed the door closed.

TJ winced. "I didn't think so," he said as the detective drove away. Then he turned to me. "What do we do now?"

"I don't know." My shoulders slumped, and suddenly I sat down in the grass and buried my face against Baxter's side. For the first time, I realized I wasn't jealous of Megan and her million lessons anymore.

I only had *this*, but this was all I wanted.

I loved Professor Reese, and I loved having her live next door. But even more than that, I *needed* her.

If I was a loser at school, that meant I was only good at two things—being a lab assistant and taking care of Baxter. If we couldn't find Professor Reese, I wouldn't have the lab anymore.

And since our landlord had a NO DOG POLICY, there was one other thing I was too scared to think about.

If we couldn't find Professor Reese, I wouldn't have Baxter, either.

21

FOR EMERGENCIES ONLY!

Me, TJ, and Baxter slumped in the yard, trying to figure out what to do. "Maybe we should ask Mom and Dad to help us," TJ said.

He had a point. But when I told him all the reasons why I didn't think we could convince the detective, I realized that we probably couldn't convince Mom and Dad, either. "And if we teleport the hat to try and prove it, and Mom sees the teleporter vibrating like crazy and then the big *POP*, there's no way she's going to let us back in the lab—she'll say it's too dangerous."

"Yeah." TJ nodded.

"Besides, if the *detective* can't find Professor Reese, and *we* can't find her, then I don't know what Mom and Dad

177

could do," I said. "Then we won't be able to get into the lab anymore, and we *still* won't have found her."

I didn't know if that was the right answer or not. I patted Baxter's ribs and thought some more. "I still feel like we can figure out where she is."

"Maybe . . ." TJ said. "I just wish she had a cell phone. Then she could call us."

"Me too." I lay back in the grass, and Baxter plunked down next to me.

Suddenly, I sat up. "Wait a minute! We could teleport a phone to her! 'Cause even though we don't know where we're sending it, it will land where she is!"

"Yeah!" TJ said. Then he frowned. "But we don't have a cell phone."

"Yes, we do!" I jumped up. "I'll be right back!"

I ran to our house and opened the front door. I could hear Mom in the kitchen, starting to cook. I sneaky quiet opened the drawer in the living room where she kept the cell phone she made me or TJ take to school when we had a field trip, in case there was an emergency.

I slipped it into my pocket and ran back outside. But when I showed it to TJ, his eyes got big.

"Jordie, we're not supposed to play with it! It's for emergencies only!"

"This is an emergency!"

I ran into Professor Reese's house and down to the lab. TJ and Baxter followed me.

I tore a sheet of paper off Professor Reese's notebook and wrote, "Call Jordie and TJ!" And I added our home phone number in case she couldn't remember it.

We opened up the lid to the teleporter and put the phone and the note in. Then I thought, Wait!

I hurried up the stairs. Baxter hurried with me.

"Where are you going?" TJ asked.

"She might be hungry. And thirsty," I yelled as I ran into the kitchen and grabbed a big bottle of water from the cupboard and two apples off the counter. "And bored!" I added as I grabbed a crossword she hadn't finished and a pen from the kitchen table.

Me and Baxter ran back downstairs, and I dumped it all in the teleporter, too. "Ready?"

TJ nodded.

So we clicked the teleporter closed, and all the equipment sprang to life—the buzzing and vibrating and then the big *POP!* Then I gave Baxter a big kiss, and me and TJ ran home.

Mom was still in the kitchen making dinner. I put my finger up to my lips to shush TJ, and we crowded around the phone in the living room, waiting for it to ring.

We waited.

And waited.

TJ slapped his forehead. "We could call *her*."

"Right!"

So TJ dialed the cell phone number, and I stuck my ear beside his so I could hear her answer, too.

But there wasn't any sound of the phone ringing on the other end. There was only static.

TJ's eyes got big. "We broke the phone!" he whispered. "Mom's going to kill us!"

"It's probably some electromagnetic thing." At least I hoped so because I didn't know how many allowances it would take to buy a new one. "Professor Reese will fix it."

He shook his head. "If we find her."

I grabbed his arm. "*When* we find her." And I decided what to do. "We are going to keep looking until Professor Reese's daughter gets here on Sunday. And if we haven't found Professor Reese by then, we'll tell *her*. 'Cause she'll believe us even though we can't prove it."

"Yeah! She's probably used to her mom doing crazy stuff!" TJ looked happy for the first time all afternoon. "OK!" He headed for his room.

"Where are you going?"

"To work on my short. It's almost dinnertime." Which TJ kept track of no matter what we were in the middle of because he's always hungry.

I suddenly realized I was starving, and my half of Baxter was probably hungry, too. I poked my head into the kitchen and told Mom that I had to feed Baxter because Professor Reese wasn't home yet. "It's a great opportunity to be dependable." Then I hurried over.

Baxter didn't meet me at the back door. I had to go all the way down to the lab to find him.

As soon as he saw me, Baxter ran over, reared up on his hind legs, and plopped his big front paws on my shoulders. We were eye to eye, then, and Baxter started to whine.

Maybe my half of Baxter was hungry, but it seemed like Professor Reese's half was trying to tell me something. "It's OK, Baxter." I nodded. "I'm listening."

He nodded back.

Baxter dropped his front paws back to the floor and ran over to the map of Portland. He parked himself down right in front of it. His crazy silver eyebrows went up and down as he looked at me and then the map and then me again. His black lips hung open, panting.

I walked over to the map and leaned in for a better look. "What are you trying to tell me?"

22

KING OF THE BOUNCE

I studied the map, stuck all over with green pins where we'd thought the hat would be, and red ones where we'd found it—always too far north or south or east or west. . . . Never where we could find it ourselves. We always had to follow Baxter.

He whined.

Professor Reese said sometimes it was good to look at things from a different angle. I lay down on the floor and stared up at the map. I stood beside it, pressing my head against the wall to look at it sideways. I put my face so close I could only focus on a tiny spot at a time. Professor Reese was right—there didn't seem to be any pattern to the pins at all.

I took a step back, then another. Then another and another until I was halfway across the room and could take in the whole map—and all the pins—in a single glance.

And suddenly it was like I was floating above the city, seeing the streets all lined up, crisscrossed like the grid on our waffle iron. Floating above the city, the pins didn't seem like the street corners where I followed Baxter as he galloped ahead. They seemed like little polka dots.

And when I hurried back to the map and stuck in one more pin in the *one place* we didn't have one (Professor Reese's house), I suddenly saw that the pins weren't random after all. They were in a pattern.

A starburst pattern.

Professor Reese's house was in the middle, and the other pins shot out from the center like a firework bursting on the Fourth of July. They shot out in tracks ending green-red, green-red, green-red—the green pin where we thought the hat would be, and then, a little farther on, and the red pin where the hat landed.

For the first time, I didn't think about us *finding* the hat, I thought about the hat *landing*. And I realized I'd always assumed that the teleporter picked up the hat and put it down someplace else.

But Professor Reese always said that a good scientist challenged assumptions, so what if my assumption wasn't right?

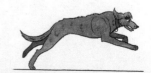

"What if the teleporter doesn't *pick up* the hat . . ." I said to Baxter.

He wagged his tail.

I studied the starburst pattern more closely. "What if the teleporter . . . *throws* it?"

He stood up and wagged harder.

"Like when I throw the superbouncy ball to you . . ."

He gave a little bark.

"That's it!" I shouted. "The hat is never where we think it will be—because the teleporter throws it, and it bounces!"

He woofed, long and loud.

"And that's why you can always find it: you're King of the Bounce!"

I wrapped my arms around Baxter and gave him a big hug (and noticed his microchip humming quieter again, which was good because his hearing would be better in a day or two and a loud hum would probably bug him). I was so happy I'd figured out the answer to one of Professor Reese's questions: that hat was never where we thought it would be because it bounced.

That still didn't tell me where Professor Reese was. "But since she teleported herself," I said to Baxter, "the more we know about teleportation, the better we can find her."

After dinner, I whispered my Bounce Theory to TJ while he took more pictures: instead of Caveman getting his brains eaten, he got up, swung his club, and knocked Zombie Cheerleader to the ground.

Then Dad came over to go with us while we took Baxter on a walk before bed. We couldn't do a Baxter Slumber Party again because that had been for one night only—Mom was afraid the landlord might stop by unannounced and catch us. But Dad said he'd go with us while we took Baxter for a walk and then sit on Professor Reese's porch and play guitar for a little while, so I could snuggle Baxter enough to last all night by himself in Professor Reese's house.

It felt sort of mysterious walking through the dark neighborhoods, with the yellow glow of lights coming out the windows of the houses and me wondering what everybody was doing in there.

TJ told Dad all about his LEGO short and how Caveman's brain was almost eaten but then wasn't.

"Wow, that sounds exciting," Dad said. "So how does it end?"

"What?" TJ asked.

"The epic battle," Dad said. "Is Caveman going to kill Zombie Cheerleader, or is Zombie Cheerleader going to kill Caveman?"

"Um . . ." TJ said, and then we all stood there quietly while Baxter stopped to sniff a little bush. "I don't know. I

haven't figured out the ending yet."

We walked back and sat on Professor Reese's porch. Dad played his guitar quietly while TJ blabbed some more. "I don't want Caveman to die. But it's really hard to kill a zombie with a club, I think."

"Aren't zombies already dead?" I asked as Baxter flopped over half on the doormat and half on me.

"*Exactly,*" TJ said.

I listened to TJ while I rubbed Baxter's tummy. Pretty soon Baxter was snoozing and making little *boop*-barking noises in his sleep. His paws started twitching, and I realized he was dreaming about running. I wondered where he was going in his dream—if he was galloping on the end of his leash, looking for Professor Reese.

TJ went on and on. "I have one hundred sixty-two pictures, which is twenty point two seconds. I still need to take seventy-eight more to make a thirty-second short. I don't want to take them until I figure out the ending." He shook his head. "But I've never made a movie before."

"Don't think of it like a movie," Dad said. "A movie tells a story. You just have to figure out how you want the story to end."

"Oh," TJ said. "OK."

Then Dad said it was time for bed. When I gave Baxter a big good-night hug, I could hear the faint hum of the microchip. But it didn't seem to be bothering him, especially with his ears still not working right. We tucked him into Professor Reese's house and went home.

Even though Professor Reese was missing, it had been a good day for me as her lab assistant because I had figured out the answer to one of her questions.

But I still needed to figure out how Baxter found the hat so far away from the house. Because it wasn't like at the dog park, when he could see the ball the whole time. We teleported the hat so far, we had to practically run for five minutes to get there. So how did he follow such a long bounce?

I pulled all my dog books off my bookcase, but none of them had a section on bouncing.

I wondered about it all night long until I fell asleep.

In the morning (Saturday = Baxterday), I woke TJ up early. We ate breakfast superfast and then left a note on the kitchen counter (because Mom was still asleep) saying we were going to go feed Baxter and take him on a walk. Then we headed over.

"But this time, when we walk," I told TJ and Baxter, "I want a plan." I nodded.

They both nodded back.

I fed Baxter and put in his ear ointment, and then we all

went downstairs to the lab. TJ said good morning to Spike (who was still gnawing on his big carrot) and plopped down in the spinny chair. Baxter plopped down on the floor beside him.

"OK." I began to pace. "We need to figure out where Professor Reese is."

"Right," TJ said.

"We just need to think through the whole thing logically."

"Right," TJ said.

"Where do you think we should start?"

"I have no idea," TJ said.

I didn't, either. But since teleportation was science, I tried to think about what a scientist might do if they were in a situation like this. "Professor Reese says that when you get new information, it's good to see how it fits in with what you already know."

"Yeah," TJ said, "but we don't have any new information."

"Sure we do." I stopped pacing so I could pat Baxter's head, but carefully so I wouldn't touch his sore ears. "We know about the bounce now."

"So?"

"So, let's look at the map again." I hurried over to it.

TJ spun in the chair. "What good will that do?"

"I don't know yet." I shrugged. "Come here anyway."

So he got up and stood by the map with me, and we looked at all the pins and the little slips of paper. I pointed to the green pin for the last time we had teleported the hat. "OK. Those are the last coordinates that we saw her type into the computer: 45.530313, –122.696471."

"Yeah, but if that's where she went, she would have just walked home," TJ said. "It's only a few blocks away."

"I know." I sighed.

We studied the map some more. And suddenly something started flitting around in the back of my mind, but I couldn't quite catch it . . .

"Wait a minute! 45.530313," TJ read again. "Where did we see that number?"

"Um . . ." I thought back. "You read it out so Professor Reese could set up the teleporter the last time we teleported the hat. And then you read it to me again later so I could write the slip."

"Yeah . . ." TJ scrunched his face up. "But didn't we see it somewhere else? I remember it because of all the threes: five three oh three one three."

And then suddenly, the idea flitting in the back of my mind stopped—and I caught hold. "That's it!"

I ran upstairs—TJ and Baxter following—through the living room through the dining room into the kitchen,

189

straight to the Baxter Station.

I grabbed the vet report, which was lying next to the ear ointment.

Then I turned to TJ and smiled. "I think we just figured it out."

23

TJ, THE GENIUS

"TJ! You're a genius!" I said.

"I am?"

I handed him the vet report. "Take a look at Baxter's microchip number."

TJ read, "45530313! I *knew* I saw that number before!" Then he scrunched up his face. "So what does that mean?"

"Hang on. Let me think—this is new information."

TJ rummaged around in his hoodie pocket. He pulled out two sticks of gum and handed one to me. I chewed and paced (and TJ just chewed).

Baxter watched me pace back and forth, first his left eyebrow going up and then his right. Pretty soon, all the little bits and pieces started fitting together, which I tried to

191

explain to TJ as I thought it through as logically as I could (in a situation like this):

- The computer sent reconfiguration instructions to the hat molecules via *radio waves.*
- Baxter's microchip number was *also* transmitted to the vet's scanner via radio waves.
- Baxter's microchip was the programmable kind.
- So *maybe* when Professor Reese's computer *beep-beep-boop*ed, Baxter *boop*ed back because his microchip was being activated and reprogrammed with a new number—the latitude for where the hat was—and the computer was telling the microchip where it needed to go.

"Wait. What?" TJ interrupted.

I stopped pacing. "I think every time she teleported the hat and the computer sent out radio waves, Baxter's microchip number changed to match where the hat was sent."

"Oh," TJ said. "So 45530313 matches 45.530313—the latitude number of the hat's coordinates from the last time we helped her teleport."

"Exactly." I nodded.

"How come the microchip doesn't show the longitude, too?"

"There's not room for all that on the LCD screen," which I just sort of made up that second, but it made sense so maybe it was right.

"Oh," TJ said.

"OK." I started pacing again. "Now, here's where it gets even crazier—"

"Good," TJ said, "because it wasn't crazy enough yet."

"So maybe," I said, "when the chip is activated, that's what makes it start humming."

"The microchip hums?" TJ asked.

"Oh! I forgot to tell you that!" I said. "Put your ear there." I pointed to Baxter's shoulder blades.

TJ did. "OK. I can hear it."

I nodded and got back to figuring things out:

- *And if* the humming grew louder the closer it got to the hat (and I'd need to test that part of my theory out), then *maybe* Baxter used the hum getting louder and louder to help him follow the bounce *all the way across town.*
- Except when Professor Reese teleported herself, Baxter's ears were messed up and he couldn't hear the humming, so he couldn't follow the bounce.
- So the fact that the microchip number written on the vet's form matched where we last sent the hat

might be a coincidence (which Professor Reese said happened a lot in scientific experiments). But it *might* be cause and effect.

"And the way to find out is to scan Baxter's microchip again," I said.

TJ looked at me for a minute. Then he said, "Huh?"

"If his microchip number *changes* every time Professor Reese plugs a new number into the teleporter, then the microchip won't have 45530313 on it anymore. It will have a *new* number now, and that will be the latitude of where she landed!"

"Oh! OK!" TJ said. Then he frowned. "But how can we scan it? We don't have a scanner."

But I was already working on a plan, which I figured I'd have figured out by the time we got to the vet's, or figured out enough that I'd just have a little bit more to figure out on the spot. So I just yelled, "Come on!" and grabbed Baxter's leash, and we all ran over there.

The receptionist remembered us from Wednesday. "How's your dog feeling?"

"Thank you for asking," I said, because it's always a good idea to be polite when you want something, plus it was just nice of her to ask. "He's doing a little bit better. But since we were in the neighborhood, we thought we'd stop in and have Dr. Sheffield check his ears again."

She looked at the appointment book. "Oh. Well, he does have a full schedule for the rest of the morning, and we close at noon on Saturdays—"

"Tell him it's the girl who wants to be a vet," I said, because I wanted to get that in before it sounded too officially like a no. "And it will just take a minute," I added, because I've noticed grown-ups have a harder time saying no when you tell them it's short.

TJ looked at me. "How will looking in his *ears* help us—" but I stomped on his foot, and he shut up.

"And it's for a report for school, and it's due Monday, so I have to do it now," I told the receptionist, because I've also noticed grown-ups always help you more if it's homework than if you just want to do something. "Please?"

She called back to his office, and he said he could squeeze us in. First we looked in Baxter's ears (which were getting better). Then I said, "So it's Career Day at school on Monday, and I have to write a report on my career, and as you know I want to be a vet" (which technically wasn't true— the report part—but I really did want to be a vet, so . . .). "And I need to do three things myself which relate to my chosen career—"

And by now TJ was just goggling at me with his eyes huge because he knew I was making everything up as I went along.

"And I can't just watch someone do them, I have to do them *myself.*" (I said that part again.) "I have already looked in Baxter's ears with an otoscope, and I have been putting ointment in them at home, so that's two things I have done myself. I need to scan his microchip for the third thing," I said. "And then I'll leave."

Dr. Sheffield must have decided it would be the quickest way to get back to his other appointments because he pulled the scanner out of the drawer and handed it to me.

TJ crowded in as I waved it over Baxter's shoulder blades. I read out, "45509091."

"Ah!" TJ yelled.

I was practically screaming, too, because that meant that it wasn't a coincidence and me and TJ had maybe discovered our first cause and effect, which is huge if you are a scientist and pretty huge even if you aren't.

But instead of screaming, I just wrote the number down. "For my report," I told Dr. Sheffield, even though secretly I was screaming inside the whole time.

TJ was staring at me with his mouth hanging open because my plan had worked. I figured we'd better leave before something dumb came out of it to give us away.

"Thank you," I said to Dr. Sheffield. Then I hustled TJ out of there.

We ran home. I tucked Baxter into Professor Reese's

house and kissed him a million times. "Be right back!"

Me and TJ went back to our house so we could look up the latitude on our computer (since Professor Reese's was password protected). TJ searched the internet and found a latitude-longitude site where you could just plug the number in. He even remembered the decimal.

"Uh-oh." TJ shook his head.

"Oh no!" I'd forgotten until that second that the latitude line cut across the whole planet—through the whole United States, plus France, Romania, and Mongolia.

"Do you think she went to Mongolia?" TJ asked.

"I don't know," I said, because it was Professor Reese, after all. "But I'm pretty sure she was planning to be home for dinner." I grabbed the mouse. "Let's see where it cuts through in Portland."

I zoomed in on the map. "The latitude line cuts through the university where she works," I said to TJ.

"And it's right by the zoo," he said back. "That would be fun—to teleport to the zoo."

We printed out the map and drew the dots where the line was, and then I yelled to Mom, "We're going back over to take care of Baxter!" and we ran out of the house.

Back in the lab, we put yellow pins (so we wouldn't mix them up with the green and red ones) across the map of Portland, showing 45.509091.

I shook my head. "It's still a big place to search—it stretches across town. And since we don't know what longitude she's at, she could be anywhere along that line."

"Yeah," TJ said. "That's going to make it a lot harder to find her."

And as I kept looking at the map, I noticed all the other things the yellow line of pins cut across, and my stomach started to tighten into a little ball.

Because Professor Reese might accidentally have teleported herself onto the freeway, into the river, or onto the railroad tracks (depending on how hard she bounced). And I really didn't want to think that getting hit by a truck, drowned in the river, or run over by a train was the reason she didn't come home.

24

3:42 A.M.

For the rest of the afternoon, TJ asked over and over, "So what are we going to do?" and I said, "Shhh! I'm thinking!" the sixth time, too.

All during dinner, TJ stared across the kitchen table at me. Every time Mom looked the other way, he made a face like, *Well?*, and I shook my head like, *Shut up or Mom will see you.*

We were so busy making faces at each other that Mom finally said, "I thought you guys liked lasagna," and I realized we hadn't been eating.

"We do!" I stuffed a big bite in my mouth, and when Mom looked away, I pointed my finger at TJ's plate like, *Eat!*

After dinner, we all, even Mom, took Baxter for a walk. I was still thinking, and, for once, TJ wasn't blabbing because he was waiting for me to finish, so Dad just whistled a tune as we walked.

"Everyone's so quiet tonight," Mom said.

Then we sat on Professor Reese's porch, while Dad played his guitar.

But this time, Baxter didn't snooze. He seemed to know that something was going on, only he didn't know quite what—which made two of us.

I looked in his eyes and whispered, "I'll tell you as soon as I figure it out, OK?"

I nodded, and he nodded back.

Then finally it was time to kiss him good night. Dad carried his guitar back to his part of the house, and me and Mom and TJ went into Mom's part.

TJ went over to his desk and just stood there, looking at Caveman and Zombie Cheerleader. I went into the bathroom and brushed my teeth. When I came out, TJ was still looking and thinking hard, it seemed, because Dad was right—a movie was a story, and TJ was figuring out how to tell it.

I went into my room. I pulled my dog books off my bookcase and sat down on the bed, wondering if they had anything in them about what it was like for a dog to miss people and to sleep in an empty bedroom listening to his own snoring when he was used to listening to someone else's.

The books said that if you wanted to understand dog feelings, you could learn a lot by looking at the behavior of wolves in the wild because dogs were descended from them. Wolves lived in packs, led by a dominant male and female. But it wasn't like they bossed everyone around. It was more like they took care of everyone and made sure they were OK. The wolf pack was a family.

Every afternoon, me and TJ and Baxter and Professor Reese were sort of like a family. We were a *pack*—and one of the pack was missing.

And that's when I figured out what me and TJ and Baxter needed to do.

So while Mom was getting ready for bed, I went into TJ's room and whispered it all to him:

In the morning, we'd get up superearly—before it was even light out—and leave a note on the counter for Mom, saying we were taking Baxter for a walk, and then we'd sneak out of the house. When she woke up a few hours later and saw the note, she'd hopefully think we'd just left (because she knew TJ didn't like to get up early). So we'd have a lot of hours—maybe three or four total—to get Baxter and walk or hopefully even gallop along 45.509091. Then we'd let the hum of the microchip getting louder lead us to Professor Reese.

TJ said, "Yeah. OK."

I said, "Don't put on your pj's. Just sleep in your clothes," which half the time he did anyway, so I figured Mom wouldn't even notice.

I put on my pj's and went into Mom's room to kiss her good night. I went back into my room and quickly wrote the taking-Baxter-for-a-walk note so it would be ready in the morning. Then I turned off the light and sneaky changed back into my clothes again.

I sat on my bed, sitting straight up so if I did fall asleep, I'd wake up when I fell over.

I looked out the window at Professor Reese's house. There was no red glow coming from the lab. There was no glow at all. It was just quiet and dark, with only Baxter all by himself, probably walking around the empty rooms sniffing how empty they were.

I looked and looked, and the street sounds got quiet. After a while, I didn't hear any cars going by anymore. Sometimes my head would start to droop, and I'd pick it back up, and then it would droop again. But I didn't fall all the way asleep because when my head konked over too much, it would wake me back up.

Then I'd look out my window again, wondering where Professor Reese was and—

I sat bolt upright in my bed. Ever since Thursday afternoon, I'd been thinking about *where* she was. But I hadn't spent any time wondering *how* she was—wherever she was.

Was she scared? Was she hurt? Because maybe she took a hard bounce. Maybe she needed help.

She needed *us*.

And even though I couldn't tell Mom about it, it was about the greatest opportunity I could ever imagine to be dependable, if I had the guts to do it:

Me and TJ couldn't wait until *morning* to head over to 45.509091 and turn right or left and listen for the hum and hope Baxter got magical again.

If she was hurt, we had to find her *now*—and there was only one way to do that.

I looked at my clock. It was 3:42 a.m. I'd never left the house in the middle of the night—but we couldn't wait any longer.

I climbed out of bed and sneaky quiet put on my sneakers (which I had never thought about until that very second, but maybe that was why they were called that).

I picked up the Baxter note.

I tiptoed past TJ's room. I didn't want to wake him until the last second because he is not exactly light on his feet. So I snuck past him on into the kitchen and laid the note on the counter. I opened the cupboard under the sink and slid out the first aid kit. Then I snuck over to TJ's bed and clamped my hand down on his mouth.

TJ's eyes flew open. I leaned in and whispered, "We have to leave now. Quiet."

When he pulled off his blanket, I saw that his shoes were already on.

We ooched the front door open and then ooched it closed. Then we snuck down the porch stairs, into the dark.

TJ whispered, "Why are we—"

But I whispered back, "Shh!" and we didn't talk until we were standing in Professor Reese's kitchen, with Baxter sleepy happy to see us and doing his just-got-out-of-bed dog stretching.

TJ pointed to the first aid kit. "Why do you have that?"

"I realized that Professor Reese may be hurt." I rummaged around the kitchen until I found a box of granola bars. I put two in my back pocket. Then I grabbed another water bottle. "I don't think we should wait all the way until morning."

TJ nodded. "OK."

"Let's check the map again." And we hurried down to the lab.

We studied the row of yellow pins where the latitude line cut through. "If she went to the zoo, she might have landed in the woods," TJ said. "So no one would see her."

"Right. There's a train station there, too, so she might have planned to get home that way."

We studied the map some more. TJ said, "But she probably went to the university."

"Yeah. 'Cause it was Thursday morning and she did have

to go to work," I said. "Maybe she aimed for a little group of trees on the edge of campus or something."

I took a deep breath. "So you head to the university—the latitude line crosses at the corner of Sixth and Jackson. And hopefully, when you get there, the humming of the microchip will be loud enough for Baxter to hear—and he'll know whether you should turn right or left," I told TJ. "But if he can't hear it yet, you'll have to put your ear down by his shoulder blades and listen to help him."

"OK," TJ said. Then he scrunched up his face. "Wait a minute. What will *you* be doing?"

"Hopefully, I'll be helping Professor Reese."

"Oh. OK." Then his eyes bugged out. "Wait! You're not going to—"

"I have to, TJ!" I said. "We don't even know for sure if you'll be able to find her—and if we wait much longer, it might be too late!"

"Why don't you just teleport the first aid kit to her?"

"I thought of that," I said. "But what if it lands where she doesn't see it? Or she can see it but can't reach it? Because it's been almost three days! Who knows what kind of shape she's in?"

I knelt down in front of Baxter and pressed my forehead against his, breathing in his sleepy-dog smell. "I'll find her, Baxter." I gave him a quick kiss for good luck, right between his ears, which were starting to get better, and his

kiss back landed on my cheek.

TJ shook his head. "I don't think you should do this, Jordie."

"I have to!" I marched over to the teleporter. "And I need you and Baxter to help." I opened the lid and put the water bottle and first aid kit at one end. "Because once I've found Professor Reese, I'll need you guys to help me get her home."

I climbed up into the teleporter, and it *was* like our waffle iron—ridged and hard and metal. "When you get to the latitude, if you can't find us, come home and tell Mom and Dad everything."

"Wait! Jordie!" TJ said.

I looked at TJ and Baxter. Everything felt way too big, and I felt way too small. But I didn't want my half of Baxter to worry about *me* for the next few hours—I needed all his whole self to get magical so he could find Professor Reese (and me too). "You help TJ, and I'll see you soon," I told him, as I lay down on the hard, metal rods. "You're a good boy!" I nodded.

Then I said what maybe Professor Reese said when she set off on her own adventure. "Here I go!"

And Baxter was still nodding as I pulled the teleporter lid down over me and clicked it closed.

25

A HARD LANDING

As soon as the lid to the teleporter clicked shut, the space around me filled with a red light, and the whole teleporter began to buzz.

A warm beam started inching from the top of my head down my face. I shut my eyes and held as still as possible, because I knew that the teleporter was scanning my molecular pattern, and I didn't want to be blurry when the instructions put me back together. It inched down my neck to my shoulders—

"Are you OK?" I heard TJ yell, over the buzzing.

But I held still as it inched across my stomach. I didn't even breathe.

"Jordie?" he yelled again.

Down my legs, over my knees, down my shins—I held still. My left foot started to itch, but it hadn't been scanned yet. I didn't scratch.

"Jordie!" TJ yelled.

Baxter woofed.

Finally, the warm beam slid past the end of my feet. "I'm OK!" I yelled back. And then the whirring started as the teleporter sent the instructions to the auxiliary computer.

About this time, I knew that Baxter was going to hide under a desk.

The whirring got louder, and I knew the other auxiliary computer was commencing T-wave generation—right . . . about . . . now!

The teleporter shuddered.

The vibrating started, and it felt jittery, like Rollerblading on a rough road. "I-I-I-I'm-m-m-m Oh-ho-ho-ho K-ay-ay-ay-ay!"

The vibrating got stronger, and the red light got redder, and the buzzing got buzzier, and the teleporter started rattling . . .

. . . and rattling . . .

. . . and rattling—

"JORDIE!"

. . . but I couldn't answer, couldn't talk anymore, couldn't breathe anymore, but who needed to breathe when you were floating and floating and floating into a million pieces of nothing and nothing and nothing . . .

. . . and maybe I heard the *POP*, but I wasn't sure because suddenly everything around me was light and windy and swirling and whooshing, and I was whooshing and whooshing . . .

. . . and maybe I felt myself drop down, and maybe I thought, The bounce . . .

. . . but then I was flying back up into the whoosh and the swirl, and then down I dropped . . .

Wham!

I felt myself pull into myself, tightening and tightening until I could feel my arms and legs and the hardness of something hard beneath me, and it took a second to remember to breathe.

And then I gasped and coughed and heard a small cry of surprise, and it was Professor Reese.

"Jordie!"

I tried to open my eyes and sit up, but I was woozy and wobbly like everything was still whooshing. "Uhhhh . . ." I groaned, and thought, This must be why Spike lay in the bottom of the hat with his feet sticking up in the air for so long.

"Lie still," Professor Reese said. "You'll feel better in a minute."

So I lay back down and closed my eyes again. "Where are we?"

"The science museum," Professor Reese said.

The spinning began to slow. I opened my eyes. Professor Reese was sitting on the floor next to me, her clothes wrinkled and her hair a mess, looking small and pale.

"Are you OK?" I said.

"Better. I'm better." She smiled weakly. "And I'm remarkably happy to see you. But, Jordie, you shouldn't have come. Teleporting is far too dangerous."

"I had to find you!" I said. "No one else would even know how to look!"

Professor Reese nodded. "That's true."

I sat up slowly and looked to see if everything was attached in the right places. Both arms had elbows and wrists and all ten fingers. My knees pointed in the right direction. I could wiggle my toes. It felt like the reconfiguration instructions worked.

Professor Reese looked attached in all the right places, too, just small and tired.

"I brought a first aid kit," I said. I looked around and saw it on the floor, the water bottle standing beside it.

"Thankfully, I'm not injured."

"And I brought water and something for you to eat." I pulled a granola bar out of my back pocket, but when she reached for it, her hand was shaking so badly, I unwrapped it for her.

"Thank you, Jordie. I was so happy to get the apples you sent, but that was many hours ago. . . ." She bit into the granola bar, closed her eyes, and chewed.

While Professor Reese ate, I looked around the little room—the concrete floor, the work sink, and in the center of the room, a huge set of shelves filled with dusty old equipment. There was a door on one wall, but all I could hear outside the room was a steady, loud whirring sound. "What is this place?"

"The storage room in the basement where I keep extra equipment. I was aiming for my office, of course, but those darn landing sites . . ."

"Oh. You bounced down here."

"What?"

So I explained all about the starburst pattern of pins on the map and discovering the bounce and how Baxter being King of the Bounce helped him find the landing sites, and Professor Reese kept saying, "Goodness!" and "Oh my!" and once, "Jordie! You figured all this out yourself?" and then, "I *knew* there was a reason I chose you as my lab assistant!"

I tried to imagine what it would be like to be stuck in this room for three whole days. There was an overhead light

but no window, so you'd just have to sit there on the hard concrete floor and try to sleep when you could. You'd be hungry, and you'd probably have to pee in the sink (that's what I would do, because who could hold it that long?). It would be lonely and a little bit scary the first few hours, I guessed, but mostly you'd just think and think, probably about how you wished you hadn't teleported yourself without first telling your lab assistants where you were going.

"Does anyone ever come in here?" I asked.

"Not very often, I would imagine," Professor Reese said. "I haven't heard anyone go by since I got here." She pulled the cell phone we'd teleported out of her pocket. "I tried calling out on this, but it doesn't work—though I do appreciate your sending it, dear."

"I think it got messed up in the teleporter."

She nodded. "Sorry about that." She took another bite of granola bar. "The first few hours in here, I tried yelling for help, but that whirring sound outside is the ventilation system for the whole building. No one heard me. And after a while, I started feeling weak."

"Well, I'm not tired. Maybe I can get us out," I said. "And hopefully TJ and Baxter will be here soon to help."

"Oh?"

"They're coming on foot because we figured it out."

I explained all about the microchip humming and

Baxter's ears and TJ recognizing the microchip number matching the latitude, and she kept saying "Oh my!" again, and her smile got bigger and bigger.

When I finished, she said, "Amazing!"

"I know! Cool, right?!"

"Very."

"OK, so let's get out of here." I went over and checked the door, but even though the doorknob turned, the door only budged a tiny bit.

"Unfortunately, it's padlocked from the outside." Professor Reese finished the granola bar. "I put the padlock on myself, a couple of years ago."

I looked around the room. There wasn't a window, and no one could hear us yell. That just left the door—padlocked from the outside.

"Maybe I can break down the door, somehow?"

I took a few steps back.

"Be careful, Jordie!" Professor Reese said.

I ran toward it as fast as I could, letting my shoulder crash into it. "Oooof!" But I just bounced back. The door didn't budge.

"Maybe I can kick the door down," I said. "I've seen that in movies." I took a few steps back and ran toward the door and kicked as hard as I could, but I just bounced back again, and now my shoulder *and* my foot hurt.

"Maybe I—"

"Enough!" Professor Reese said. "Let's use our noggins. And I don't mean headbutting the door."

So I walked over to the shelves in the middle of the room. "What's all this stuff?"

"Scientific apparatus from the eighteenth through the early twentieth centuries. This is where I store the equipment I'm not using in the displays upstairs."

There were all kinds of crazy equipment with little parts bolted together: small glass domes, big glass beakers, disks with tiny arrows and *Volts* stamped across the front, small cranks and big cranks, pulleys and pipes and thick glass lenses. Everything looked like it could have been in Frankenstein's laboratory or maybe a pirate ship.

On the bottom shelf was a big jumble of coiled wire and old rubber tubing and a funny-looking microscope. "Is that a spectrometer?" I asked.

Professor Reese beamed. "It is! I'm so pleased you recognized it!"

"We can't use it somehow to get out of here, can we?"

She shook her head. "Unfortunately, no."

I walked around behind the shelves. Back in the corner of the room, sitting on a wheelie cart, was a big metal ball with a hand crank attached to it. "Hey! There's one of those TJ zappers, just like the one in the Physics Lab!"

"A Van de Graaff generator, yes," Professor Reese said. "Sometimes when we have a large school group, we bring it upstairs and split the group into two teams. Then we have a competition to see which team can crank the fastest to generate the most electricity."

"Oh, cool!" I said. "But that can't get us out of here, either, right?"

Professor Reese shook her head. "I don't see how."

I walked around the room, looking at things up close and far away, from the right and from the left. But no matter how many angles I looked at everything from—even if I stood on my head—I couldn't think of any way out of that room.

I went over to the door, sat down, and leaned against it. "I have one more granola bar. Do you want it?"

Professor Reese came and sat down next to me. "I think we'd better save it for later . . ." She didn't say any more, but she didn't have to. I knew what she was thinking:

All we could do was wait—and hope that TJ and Baxter found us.

CRANKING THE
TJ ZAPPER

Me and Professor Reese sat, leaning against the door, waiting and hoping for TJ and Baxter.

Then we sat some more and hoped for TJ and Baxter even harder. "What do we do if they can't find us?" I asked.

"Don't say that," Professor Reese answered. "They will."

I didn't think it would be possible to get sleepy, but after a while my head kept konking over until finally I rested it on Professor Reese's shoulder and let myself drift off . . .

A *tap-tap-tap* on the other side of the door jolted me awake. "Jordie?" I heard TJ say.

Baxter whined.

"TJ! Baxter!" Professor Reese cried. "You found us!"

"Yeah, you were right, Jordie," TJ said. "Baxter's

microchip did start humming louder and louder. Once we got near the river, he was able to follow the humming all the way here!"

"Good boy, Baxter!" I said.

Baxter woofed.

"But how did you get into the building?" Professor Reese asked. "Did someone let you in?"

"6-5-4-3-2-1 blast off!" TJ answered. "I remembered the code number for the employee door. I don't think anyone's here yet. It's still early."

"Good work," Professor Reese said. "Unlock the padlock and get us out of here!"

"OK!" But then a second later, TJ added, "This is a weird lock."

"It's an electronic padlock," Professor Reese said. "I couldn't resist. I set the combination myself: 9-22-1791." She turned to me. "Michael Faraday's birthday."

"Who's that?" I asked.

"A British physicist. One of the pioneers of electromagnetism."

"OK, hang on a sec. . . ." TJ said.

Baxter stuck his nose down at the small crack beneath the door. He sniffed and sniffed, so I stuck my finger through the little gap so he could sniff it better. He whined. He missed us.

"The lock doesn't work," TJ said.

Professor Reese frowned. "It's powered by a battery. The buttons should light up blue when you punch the numbers in."

"Nothing is lighting up."

"The battery must be dead." Professor Reese sighed. "You'll have to wait until the museum opens, and then bring someone down to let us out, TJ."

"But how will you explain how we got in here? The door is locked from the outside!" I said. "If you tell people about the teleporter, it won't be a secret anymore."

"True," she said. "But we have to get out of here."

"Wait a minute." I stood up. "You always say when you get new information, it's good to see how it fits into what you already know, right?"

"True. But what new information do we have?"

"We still have a locked door, only now TJ and Baxter are on the other side of it," I said. "So things aren't the same anymore."

"Good point." Professor Reese nodded. "Let's think about this." She closed her eyes for a minute. Then she opened them. "If the padlock battery is dead, there's a way to recharge it enough to unlock the lock."

"Good!" TJ said. "How?"

"Do you see the little handle at the bottom of the lock?

Pull down on that."

"Hang on. . . ." TJ said. "OK, it's open."

"That's a battery jump slot," Professor Reese told him. "We can insert a fresh battery into the slot to power the padlock."

"Good!" TJ said. "Do you have a fresh battery? You can slide it under the door."

I looked around. "Maybe. There's a lot of stuff in here."

So me and Professor Reese looked all over the shelves, from the top to the bottom. But the shelves were filled with old equipment, and none of it used a battery.

Professor Reese's shoulders slumped. "No luck, TJ. I guess we'll just have to wait until the museum opens."

She sat down on the floor, leaned against the wall, and closed her eyes.

But I wasn't ready to sit yet. I walked back and forth across the room and thought, Since science got us stuck in here, maybe science can get us out. "It seems like with all these domes and beakers and cranks and pulleys and pipes, there should be *something* we can do."

From the other side of the door, Baxter whined.

"What *is* a battery, anyway?" I asked Professor Reese, because I realized just then that I didn't really know.

"A battery converts stored chemical energy into electrical energy," she said.

Baxter whined louder.

"OK, so a battery gives off electricity. That makes sense." I looked at the shelves. "Can't we *make* a battery with all of this equipment? Or the TJ zapper?"

Baxter woofed!

Professor Reese's eyes flew open. "The Van de Graaff generator! Jordie, I have never been more proud of you than I am at this moment! And never more grateful to have you as my lab assistant. You and TJ both!" She stood up. "We don't need to make a battery—I think we might be able to generate enough electrical energy to unlock the padlock!" She hurried around the big shelves to the back corner of the room. "Come help me, dear!"

She took hold of one end of the cart, and I took hold of the other.

"What's going on?" TJ asked.

"I think we're going to use the TJ zapper to make electricity!" I said as we wheeled it over to the door.

"There's a zapper in there?" TJ asked.

While I told him about all the stuff on the shelves, Professor Reese untangled a long piece of rubber tubing and a small coil of wire from the bottom shelf. She slid one end of the wire all the way through the tubing until it stuck out the other end. "The wire will carry the charge, and the tubing will work as insulation."

She fed the rubber-covered wire under the door. "Pull that toward you, TJ. You'll need about five feet in order to reach up to the lock." She turned to me. "Wrap the other end of the wire around the big ball, Jordie. Since your end isn't covered in rubber, it will conduct the charge."

At first, I was scared to touch the ball. But then I remembered that the zapping didn't start until you turned the crank. "OK!" I wrapped the wire around and around until the ball looked a little bit like a globe covered in latitude lines.

"Put the tip of the wire into the battery slot, TJ," Professor Reese said. "I'll hold the tubing still." She turned to me. "Jordie, start cranking!"

So I cranked and cranked and then cranked some more.

"It's working!" TJ cried. "The lights on the padlock are lighting up!"

"Punch in the combination, quick!" I yelled. "My arms are getting tired!"

"9-22-1791!" Professor Reese added.

I cranked and cranked until I thought my arms were about to fall off, with Baxter woofing to cheer me on.

Just when I thought I couldn't crank anymore, TJ yelled, "It worked!"

The door opened, and Baxter rushed in. I let go of the crank and let him crash into me. "You found us, Baxter!

Good boy!" I nodded extra hard.

Baxter nodded back.

Both halves of Baxter wiggled crazy happy to see Professor Reese and crazy happy to see me. Professor Reese patted him, while I gave him a big hug. Sure enough, the microchip had stopped humming. Baxter had gotten where he needed to go.

"Let's get out of here!" TJ said.

So we closed the door (but this time we were on the other side of it) and put the padlock back on.

"There's an elevator over here," Professor Reese said. She walked so slowly that I unwrapped the other granola bar and handed it to her, and we just kept moving forward at half-starved-physicist speed until we were into the elevator. I pushed the button for the ground floor.

The elevator door opened up into the Turbine Hall. Outside, the sun was already up, and joggers were starting to pass by.

I knew we wouldn't be able to walk all the way home— Professor Reese was too weak. "Do you think you can make it to the streetcar platform?" I asked as we crossed the hall and left through the employee entrance.

Professor Reese nodded and gripped my arm. TJ and Baxter led the way.

We waited at the far end of the streetcar platform, which

would be the last car of the streetcar, farthest from the driver. And when the streetcar got there, we just sort of slipped on with the other passengers. Technically, there was a sign that said *All Dogs Must Be in Carriers*, but untechnically, Baxter was better behaved than some of the *people* on the streetcar (seriously, I swear) and besides, a carrier big enough to fit Baxter would have had to be the size of a car, practically, and then we just could have driven. Nobody seemed to mind him being there, anyway, and most people even liked it.

So everything was working out fine, and I started thinking how it had turned into a great day. After we got Professor Reese settled back at her house, we'd be able to go back to our house before Mom noticed we'd been gone long enough to get worried.

We crossed the bridge and got out at the transfer station and then transferred from the blue to the green line. When we climbed onto the green line streetcar, I finally leaned back in my seat and felt myself relax, because we were almost home.

But just as the streetcar doors were closing, I looked out the window and saw Detective John Jacobs of the Portland Police Department (who I had totally forgotten about, and who was just climbing into his car with a cup of coffee, probably about to drive up to Professor Reese's house

again). He was staring right at me and TJ and Baxter, who had his nose pressed up against the glass. I could see the gears turning in his head as he tried to figure out if the little old lady sitting next to us was who he *thought* it was.

I slumped down in my seat, wondering if it was too late to pretend I hadn't seen him. But just as the streetcar started to move, TJ stood up, waved both arms above his head, and cried, "Hey! We found her!"

Detective John Jacobs's eyes practically popped out of his head, and I knew at that moment that he'd be waiting on Professor Reese's front porch when we got home, and that meant we only had a short streetcar ride to figure out what in the world we were going to tell him.

27

MUTANT FROGS AND NUCLEAR ANTS

The rest of the way home on the streetcar, we tried to figure out what to tell Detective John Jacobs—because we knew he'd be expecting answers.

Professor Reese said, "Maybe I should tell him I got so busy at work that I didn't notice the time."

"But for three whole days?" I said. "It doesn't seem believable that nobody else at work would have seen you when they were all worried and looking for you."

"Wait! How about this!" TJ said. "We say you were kidnapped by bandits who came in on a helicopter while you were going to work on Thursday morning. They grabbed you from behind and tied you up and stuffed a sock in your mouth." He sat up a little bit more in his seat. "Yeah,

a sock. A dirty one. They flew you to their secret hideout in the jungle with vines growing all over the front of it so no one could see it. There were snakes in the vines that could kill you in a *single bite* and spiders—big spiders—" He spread his hands wide to show how big. "No, wait, *tarantulas*, the big hairy kind, crawling all over the walls inside the hideout. And *that* was only if you could get past the attack Dobermans whose fangs were dripping blood from their last victims . . ."

TJ went on and on as we got off the streetcar and walked through the neighborhood back to Professor Reese's house, but his idea didn't seem very believable, either, and by the time he was finished telling it to us, we were out of time.

But as we helped Professor Reese up the front walk, with Detective John Jacobs standing on the porch with his arms crossed, glaring at us—I suddenly knew, and I whispered, "Don't worry, I have it all figured out."

I'd figured out that the best thing to tell him was *the truth* because you should never lie to a policeman, even one as crabby as Detective John Jacobs. Besides—when Detective John Jacobs barked out, "Just where have you been? I have *a report* to fill out, you know!" and I said, "Professor Reese teleported herself to the science museum, and my magical dog helped find her," and Professor Reese smiled and said it was true, he muttered, "*Un*believable!"

Then he stomped to his car and drove away. Just like I thought he would.

I helped Professor Reese upstairs. While she was in the shower, I came back down and made peanut butter and jelly sandwiches and cut up apples, and TJ made cracker stacks for everyone, even Baxter.

And then Professor Reese came downstairs looking better, and we ate together. First Professor Reese told us what it was like when she teleported and landed in the pitch-black storage room. "At first, I must admit, I panicked because I couldn't see anything, and I wondered if teleporting made you blind," she said. "But after I calmed down and explored my surroundings, I realized that I might just be in a dark room. I crawled until I found the wall and then felt around for the door, and then I stood up and found the light switch." She shook her head and smiled. "I felt much better after that."

I told her and TJ what it felt like when I teleported, and Professor Reese and I agreed that the landing was pretty hard. "We'll have to work on that," she said.

We all ate a little bit more, and suddenly I remembered, "Oh! Your daughter is flying in from Australia this afternoon."

Professor Reese got all excited and happy, and then we noticed the light on her answering machine was blinking,

and it was six calls from her daughter, each one sounding more worried and the last one saying she was flying to Portland and landing on Sunday at 2:47 p.m. and would take a cab straight over.

"Are you going to tell her what really happened?" TJ asked.

Professor Reese nodded slowly. "I suppose I'll have to. She'll be angry that I took such a big risk teleporting myself—but she's my family. She loves me, and she deserves to know."

"Professor Reese?" I said. "When you tell your daughter, can we tell my parents, too, even though it's supposed to be a secret? 'Cause they'll be mad that me and TJ didn't tell them what was going on, and that I teleported, and that TJ walked across town in the middle of the night and snuck into the science museum to get us—" And when I listed it all in a row like that, I started getting nervous at just how mad Mom and Dad were going to get.

"They love you," Professor Reese said, "and they deserve to know, too."

I nodded.

And so we worked it out that when Professor Reese's daughter got there, Professor Reese would invite me and TJ and Mom and Dad over, and we could tell everyone at the same time and all get in trouble together instead of each of us getting in trouble separately, which always feels worse.

"And now, my dears, I need to lie down for a little while."

TJ looked at the clock. "We'd better go over to Dad's. It's already waffle time."

And even though I'd just eaten, I knew I still had a little bit of room for half a waffle, and TJ probably had room for a whole. "OK, tell him I'll be over in a minute."

TJ grabbed an apple slice and ran down to the lab to give it to Spike, and I helped Professor Reese upstairs, with Baxter leading the way.

"It must be a relief knowing you won't have to save any little old ladies tomorrow," she said as I helped her into bed. "You can just go to school and have fun."

"Yeah." Then I remembered that tomorrow was Monday. "Well, I'll have fun on Tuesday. Tomorrow I have to go hide in the stupid bathroom."

"Oh my. Why is that?"

So I told her the rest of what had happened in Study Buddies and how I thought Mrs. A. chose me first because of my excellent people skills, but really she just thought I was *unfocused*. "And the whole time I thought I was helping Katie and Maya."

"You know," Professor Reese said, patting my hand, "scientists usually review *all* the data they've gathered before

drawing any conclusions." She lay back on her pillows. "And now, I really must take a nap."

I tiptoed out of the room, past Baxter—who was snoring on his smooshy dog bed—and down the stairs. TJ had left, so I washed the dishes and then closed the front door behind me.

But I didn't want to go over to Dad's—not yet. I knew that he was probably mixing the waffle batter, and TJ had probably turned on Dad's TV to watch some dumb movie about giant mutant frogs or a colony of crazed nuclear ants that march across whole towns eating every living thing and leaving skeletons behind with their skull jaws open, screaming because ants are crawling out their eye sockets.

Before I sat down to watch with him, I wanted five minutes of peace and quiet.

I wandered over to the middle of the park and sat down beneath a tree. To my left was the dog playground, where Baxter was King of the Bounce. To my right were the basketball courts, where Tyler was already out shooting hoops.

I wanted to think about what Professor Reese had just said: that a scientist reviews *all* the data before drawing any conclusions.

Before I'd done Study Buddies, I'd assumed Tyler was the worst kid in the whole class. But now I knew him a lot better.

He got in trouble in class all the time. And he told *way* too many butt jokes. But he was also funny and nice to dogs and nice to other kids. And he'd turned into an outstanding Study Buddy in the end.

Tyler said Mrs. A. thought we were both losers. But, I realized, she'd never *said* that. When I looked at all the data I'd gathered about Tyler, he didn't seem like a loser. And if Tyler wasn't a loser, did that mean maybe I wasn't one, either?

As I watched him make a shot, I wondered, What if *neither one of us* is a loser?

Maybe I was a tiny bit unfocused—or at least, not focused on what Mrs. A. wanted me to focus on—because I did sort of whisper a lot when she was starting her lessons. But if I'd been *too* focused—as focused as Detective John Jacobs—I never would have looked at things from a different angle and figured out how the teleporter worked or how Baxter followed the bounce or anything.

And in Study Buddies, I'd helped Maya be a little less shy and Katie be a little less sticky—and that was pretty good for only two weeks.

So when I looked at all the data I'd gathered about *myself,* it didn't seem very loser-y at all.

I didn't realize I'd been holding my breath until it came out in a big sigh, like the kind of sigh Baxter made when

he flopped down next to me, cozy and warm—a sigh like he knew he'd found a really good home.

I could hear Tyler's basketball thumping as he dribbled it across the court. He faked left, went right, and nailed it.

"Nice shot," I called out.

He looked over, surprised. "Uh, thanks." He charged the net and nailed a layup, too.

Then I stood up to head to Dad's—because if TJ was facing giant mutant frogs and flesh-eating nuclear ants, he could probably use some company.

28

A PINK BOX THE SIZE OF SOMETHING DELICIOUS

When the phone rang at five thirty, I let Mom get it. I heard her say, "Oh! I'm so glad you're all right!" and then, a minute later, "Why, yes, that would be lovely. Are you sure there's nothing we can bring?"

Professor Reese had invited us to dinner to explain why she'd been missing, Mom told me and TJ after she hung up the phone. So I ran to get Dad, who had just gotten home from the music store, and we all trooped over to Professor Reese's house.

Her daughter, Lydia, was there, and she was very nice and looked just like Professor Reese, only with brown hair, not gray, and without the wrinkles.

I smiled at Baxter, and he grinned back.

As soon as we sat down in the living room, the doorbell rang and it was the pizza delivery boy, so we all moved into the dining room. And just as we were getting our pizza and salad, the doorbell rang again. Lydia went to answer it and came back with a pink cardboard bakery box the size of something delicious. TJ's eyes got big, and I could tell he was excited.

While we ate, Professor Reese explained all about T-waves and promised to demonstrate teleportation to prove it. And when Lydia said, "Mom!" Professor Reese added, "I'll prove it with the *hat*, not *myself*!"

Mom and Dad and Lydia promised not to tell anyone else about the teleportation experiments because it was Professor Reese's announcement to make when she was ready.

"But I'll be ready soon," Professor Reese said, "and that's because of the fine work of my lab assistants, who aren't just assistants anymore—they're truly scientists now."

I explained how the hat bounced and the microchip number changed and how if Baxter wasn't King of the Bounce, we never would have been able to help Professor Reese with her scientific discovery.

"*Our* scientific discovery," Professor Reese said. "You and TJ have made a real contribution to science."

"And Baxter," I added.

"And Spike!" TJ said. Then he explained all the parts about the latitude numbers and helping Baxter follow the hum to the science museum—

"Hold on, TJ," Mom interrupted. "When did you go to the science museum with Baxter?"

"Um," TJ said. He stuffed a big bite of pizza into his mouth and looked at me, like, *You tell them that part.*

I took a deep breath. "Yeah, well, I had a whole bunch of great opportunities to be dependable because Professor Reese was counting on me." Only the more I told the opportunities, one by one, the less great they sounded. Mom's eyebrows got higher and higher, and pretty soon no one was eating anymore, not even TJ, just waiting for me to finish them all. Lydia and Dad were shaking their heads.

And when I finished, for about five minutes everyone was talking all at once, and boy, did me and TJ get an earful—though Mom and Dad finally did admit that if we *had* tried to tell them about teleportation without Professor Reese there to back us up, they wouldn't have believed it, because, seriously, who would?

But even though Lydia and Mom and Dad were really mad, they weren't completely and totally mad because mixed in with all the stuff we got in trouble for were a lot of great things, too—like Professor Reese inventing

teleportation but me and TJ being the ones who figured out how it worked. Plus, us being able to find her when no one else could, and also us maybe even keeping her from starving to death a little bit.

So all that was really impressive and made Mom and Dad and Lydia at least a little bit less mad.

I winced. "So how long are me and TJ grounded for?"

Dad shook his head. "This is *way* bigger than being grounded," he said. "This is the biggest thing ever, Jordie: we're a *family*, and families look out for each other."

"Like a wolf pack," I said.

"Well, yes, exactly: like a wolf pack," Mom said. "And your dad and I can't look out for you and TJ when you don't tell us what's going on."

Mom looked long and hard at TJ and even longer and harder at me. She even looked long and hard at Professor Reese. "Agreed?"

We all nodded. And when I looked over at Baxter, he was nodding, too.

"So we're *not* grounded?" TJ added and flashed Mom and Dad a big grin, like, *Pleeeeease?*

Everyone laughed.

So the day turned out great (even though it had started out really exhausting). Plus, inside the pink box was cake.

Professor Reese told us that after her nap, she'd called

around to find a bakery that delivered. And it was the greatest cake I'd ever seen because it was huge and chocolate and had *My Heroes* written on it (in purple frosting to match Baxter's collar), and the heroes were me and TJ and Baxter.

"I think you only invented a teleporter so you can see your grandkids more often," Lydia said and laughed as she cut the cake.

"It did occur to me." Professor Reese smiled and started passing the cake plates.

"You have grandkids?" I said.

"Yes, a boy and a girl, only the boy is the one who's a year older."

"Ha!" TJ said.

Once we all had our cake in front of us, Professor Reese put a slice of pizza on another plate and placed it on the floor for Baxter, since dogs can't have chocolate.

"There's only one thing I'm wondering about," I said, watching him wolf it down (which was still not as messy as TJ wolfing down *his* pizza, even though TJ is the one who can actually pick it up since he has thumbs). "If Baxter just follows the hum of his microchip, does that mean he's *not* magical?"

Baxter turned toward us, and his crazy silver eyebrows went up and down as he looked back and forth among us all.

Professor Reese thought about it a minute. Then she smiled. "Well, who would have ever guessed that the key to unlocking one of the greatest scientific advances in the history of mankind would be a shaggy gray dog named Baxter—King of the Bounce."

She dug her fork into her cake. "That seems a little bit magical to me."

29

PRETTY OUTSTANDING AT THE END

In the morning, I ran over to Professor Reese's as soon as I finished my Crispy Rice. TJ was still eating his so slowly that it would be a bowl of slimy mush at the end (seriously), and I wanted to get there early.

I rang the doorbell, and Baxter started woofing. His ears were getting better.

Lydia answered the door. "Hi, Jordie!"

Baxter nosed his way past her and licked my hands, his tail wagging so hard he practically fell off his own back feet. I kissed the spot between his eyebrows, and Baxter kissed me back, between mine.

I went into the living room. Professor Reese was wearing a silvery-gray leotard and gray tights, looking a little bit

like Baxter. "Good morning, dear," she said, writing *octagonal* in 23-down (for "having eight sides").

"How are you feeling?" I asked.

She patted her stomach. "Much better. I'm stuffed! Lydia has been spoiling me silly."

"I like taking care of you," Lydia said. She kissed the top of Professor Reese's head, which was nice, because even when you are all grown up you are still somebody's mom and somebody's daughter. Then she went into the kitchen.

"So, Jordie," Professor Reese said, "what did you decide—are you still going to hide in the bathroom today?"

I scritched Baxter's shaggy gray chin. "No. I decided that I really was a pretty outstanding Study Buddy."

Professor Reese nodded. "Good."

Then TJ got there, and the whole way to school, he was all excited because he'd just figured out how his short was going to end.

He was going to let Spike go scuttling across the set toward where Caveman and Zombie Cheerleader were fighting, and since Spike was as big as they were, he'd look like Godzilla Cockroach. So Godzilla Cockroach would chase Caveman and Zombie Cheerleader, and they would run away.

So in TJ's story, everyone lived (if you count being a zombie as living) to fight another day. "And," TJ said, "then I can make a sequel!"

He was so excited that as soon as we got to school, he ran off to find his friends and tell them.

But when I reached the edge of the school playground, my stomach started feeling fluttery. Because it was *one* thing to decide you weren't a loser after all but *another* thing for everyone else to decide it, too.

Across the blacktop, Megan and Aisha and Jasmine were at the bars, balancing and spinning around backward.

I stopped and held my breath.

Megan looked my way . . . and gave me a huge smile.

She started running toward me.

I ran up to meet her. "How was your recital?"

"It was OK," she said. "But that's not the exciting thing. The *really* exciting thing is that after the recital, I told my mom I didn't want to take piano anymore, and she said fine. She said *she* always thought *I* was the one who wanted to take it!" Megan laughed. "So now I can start coming over to your house every week to help you with Baxter!"

"He'll love that!" I said. "And I will, too!"

We hurried together toward the bars. Aisha and Jasmine both hopped down and grabbed their backpacks.

I thought, Oh no, are they leaving?

But instead, Aisha unzipped the zipper on the front pocket and pulled out her notebook. "Jordie! Look what I made!"

It was a sketch of me . . . with my arm around Baxter!

"I based Baxter on that drawing I did, right after you got him." She smiled. "Remember when you were telling me his ears were longer and his eyebrows were crazier?"

"Yeah!" I said as she tore it out of her notebook and handed it over. "It looks just like us!"

"I thought of another thing I could do at the vet/beauty parlor/day care," Aisha said. "I can make portraits of the kids with their dogs!"

"And I can raise the money for the art supplies," Jasmine added. "Because look what me and my mom made!" She unzipped the top of her backpack and pulled out a plastic bag, only instead of scones or breakfast bars, there were these little dog bone–shaped cookies. "I made dog biscuits! We can sell them at the vet part!" She handed the bag to me. "These are peanut butter, but I found a bunch of recipes online. Tell Baxter I can make other flavors, too!"

I thought, Yay! No one thinks I'm a loser! They *didn't* forget all about the vet/beauty parlor/day care the minute they got home—they'd been thinking about it all weekend!

Soon we were blabbing so much that we decided to do a big slumber party together and invite Baxter, too, so it would be a Baxter Slumber Party. "We have a family room in the basement," Jasmine said. "And my mom loves dogs."

"I'm pretty sure Professor Reese will let her half of Baxter spend the night," I said. "And I know mine can!"

So the day started great, and when morning recess came around, it stayed that way. Me and Tyler (going to say good-bye) and Danica and Robert (going to say hello) went up one hallway and down the other. As we walked, Tyler gave Robert advice (like how to do bounce-pass keep-away) and shared helpful insider tips (like how Mrs. Wilson didn't like fart jokes, but you could probably get away with a butt joke or two). Me and Danica just rolled our eyes.

When we got to Room Six, I gave Maya and Katie each a big hug. "I'll come play with you whenever I see you on the school playground."

They were so excited they bounced up and down. And even though I wasn't their Study Buddy anymore, I was still their buddy, so I bounced, too.

"Here!" Katie handed me a big card.

"We made it for you!" Maya bounced again.

They'd drawn a picture of all three of us on the front. When I opened it up, it said, "Thank you, Jordie! We LOVE you!!!" and they had written *LOVE* so big that they had to run the *you* down the side of the card, but I didn't care because it was perfect.

"I'll put this up in my room at home and look at it every day," I told them.

And when Mrs. Wilson told me what an awesome Study

Buddy I'd been, I believed her. Because I had.

So the day stayed great, because after school there were *two* cherry Popsicles left in the box (for once in my life, I swear).

And when me and TJ went over to Professor Reese's house, she had a little sparkle in her eyes, like she'd thought up a new experiment and would be needing the help of her lab assistants. And who knew what we'd get to do?

"We're ready for anything," I told her as I scritched Baxter's shaggy gray neck and added some pets and pats. "Right, Baxter?"

I nodded three times, up and down.

And Baxter nodded back.

ACKNOWLEDGMENTS

A great big THANK-YOU to my editors, Nancy Inteli and Cheryl Eissing; all the folks at HarperCollins, including production editor Emily Rader and designer Rick Farley; copy editor Jennifer Lattanzio Moles; and my agent, Jodi Reamer.

A huge HOORAY to my family, Scott, Anna, and Seamus.

And to my writing buddies—Liz, Emily, Ellen, Kim, Nancy, Ruth, Carmen, Kessa, April, Suz, Jennifer, Stephen, Mary, Tash, JoAnn, Deb, and Genny—the next round of cupcakes is on me.